SMILE FOR THE PRETTY LADY

As we drew closer I tried to think of something friendly to say, something that would get us on our way as quickly as possible without being impolite. But she didn't seem to notice my efforts. Her wide eyes fixed upon me as her teeth clenched down in a rigid jaw. As she got closer I noticed her left arm pressing the purse tight against her breasts. Her right hand was inside the purse, grabbing for something.

Then she withdrew her fist, and clutched tightly in it was a Colt's revolver. Her eyes were cold and locked unblinking upon my face. My breath caught in my throat, and I froze there on the sidewalk, too stunned to move.

"This is for Joey," she said.

Those were the last words I heard as she pulled the trigger . . .

Praise f

"*Cripple Creek* capture
frontier."

—Fred Bean

"A two-fisted winner! Doug Hirt is a unique talent . . . a real page-turner."

—Giles Tippette

THE WRONG MAN

DOUGLAS HIRT

THE WRONG MAN

A Berkley Book / published by arrangement with
the author

PRINTING HISTORY
Berkley edition / June 2000

The Penguin Putnam Inc. World Wide Web site address is
http://www.penguinputnam.com

ISBN: 0-425-17502-2

BERKLEY®
Berkley Books are published
by The Berkley Publishing Group,
a division of Penguin Putnam Inc.,
375 Hudson Street, New York, New York 10014.
BERKLEY and the "B" logo are trademarks
belonging to Penguin Putnam Inc.

PRINTED IN THE UNITED STATES OF AMERICA

10 9 8 7 6 5 4 3 2 1

1

"CALICO LACE."

The words seemed somehow out of place on that weather-beaten sign, standing bold and forthright against the wind and snow of these mountains. I would have thought Ramrod, or Iron Town, or Poverty Gulch a more fitting name for a place shaped up out of the side of this mountain; all rock and heavy logs, with sidewalks knee-high off the road to accommodate the winter snows. But there it was, what still could be read of the flaking paint. Calico Lace.

"Reckon someone must have a sense of humor." I pondered while my horse snorted and pawed the dust of the road. It was an odd name, but then I've heard of and been to stranger places.

Beside me astride his wide roan, McGee stroked the coarse red stubble of his chin and shaded his eyes toward the town. Calico Lace was hunkered down on the sunny side of the mountain slope, whose cold and naked peak shoved against a cloudless Colorado sky maybe ten miles farther on, and another five thousand feet higher up. It was a rocky, unfriendly jut of real estate, scored by the ages and creased deep where winter's snow would lie shingle-deep to a hardscrabble's soddy until long into springtime.

He licked his cracked lips with a dry tongue and said, "Wonder how it got such a name."

"Let's find out."

"Reckon this here Calico Lace place has got itself a saloon, Cap? Someplace fittin' to wash down the gravel of this last week, and get us oiled up real good for the next?"

Cap. I hardly even heard it anymore. McGee had been calling me that since we first met. By now it was as much my name as was the one my father gave me: Jacob Kellogg. Maybe more. McGee and me, we've ridden together a lot of years. I grinned at my friend and steadied my anxious horse with a hand to its neck.

"Haven't met a town yet that didn't have at least one saloon."

McGee grinned back and we clucked our horses forward.

The tall pines had been hacked away from the town, leaving a wide swath of hard, rocky ground where sunlight reached down and warmed the two dozen or so rough-hewn buildings. The main street was a dry, dusty strip, but come the next good rain it would be one long mud hole.

Horses nosed at the hitching rails, batting flies with their tails while folks moved along those high sidewalks, giving us the eye as we rode in.

"You'd think they never seen strangers before," McGee noted.

"They are just curious," I said. At first glance Calico Lace seemed a friendly place to spend some time and money. Not that we ever had much in the way of money. It was like a hundred other towns McGee and I have passed through, scattered haphazardly across the West. To my right I spied a barbershop. Watching the fellow through the window lathering up the chin of a gent in a tall, straight-back chair, I remembered I could use a shave too. The barber happened to glance up just then and the brush stopped. He spoke to the man in the chair, who bolted around and glared out the window at us like we were a couple Apaches riding through. We'd been four or five days in the saddle since Glenwood Springs, it's true, but I didn't figure we looked all *that* bad.

"There it be, Cap."

McGee's words pulled my eyes off the two men. I gave a wry grin and wondered if maybe McGee was right. Maybe they didn't get many strangers through here after all. We turned our horses into the rail in front of Millford's Saloon and dismounted. Folks seemed suddenly scarce around the saloon. A tightness pulled at my shoulders as a thumbnail dragged up my spine.

"Business appears to have fallen off," I said.

"Folks acting a mite peculiar in this here Calico Lace town, Cap."

"They do seem right nervous about something."

McGee smirked. "I get this feeling it's you and me they are shying from. We ever been here afore?"

"No." I'd already asked myself that question. We'd

stopped counting towns years ago, but even that was a long time after McGee and I had started riding together. McGee had been my first sergeant during the war. After Lee handed his sword over to Grant in '65, I returned to Ohio, and McGee just tagged along with me. I never got around to asking why and he never volunteered a reason. He had no family, no home. That was reason enough for some men after four years of killing. I was about the only family he had, so we rode together.

He stayed with me during those hard times after the war, as I cleared up all the loose ends of a shattered life. When I'd finished and had sold off what was left of the farm, he swung up onto his horse beside me and peered long and sadly at the charred remains that had once been Betty's and my home.

"Ain't much left here for you, Cap," he had said.

I could only shake my head. I had already cried out all the tears I had inside me.

"Got any plans?"

He knew I didn't. How could anyone have plans when their whole life lay buried in cold graves? I had had plans once. Large, grand plans like most young men rolling up their sleeves, eager to tackle a bold world with a beautiful wife at their side, and newborn twins in their arms. But then came the war . . . and other things—things that play hell with a man's life. Betty and the twins were my life. Now they were gone and I knew it was going to take a good long time to get things straightened out again—a good long time to forget.

"No, no plans."

"I hear there is a big empty country over beyond the

Mississippi just begging for men to fill her up."

So we started west. No place in particular. Any place would do; any place where I could put the past far behind me. And all the while McGee rode at my side. I never asked why. I was grateful for the company, although I don't think I ever told him so. He just seemed to know.

That had been well over ten years ago. More than a decade since I laid my life in those graves. A dozen years and too many jobs and lonely towns between to count. And as I thought on it now, standing there in front of Millford's Saloon, in this little mountain town of Calico Lace, I still had no plans for my life.

"I'm thinking maybe we should take that drink and then move on a piece, huh? I'm starting to feel like that time we come onto that Comanches camp down on the Purgatorie, Cap."

McGee's words stirred me from my thoughts. McGee was a short, husky fellow; strong as a mule and hardly ever spooked. He had pale blue eyes, ruddy skin, and a tangle of red hair like a ball of rusty baling wire that someone had tried to squeeze into the brim of a tattered Stetson.

"This isn't the first town that hasn't sent out a brass band to welcome us," I said, glancing at the lengthening shadows reaching across the street to where a lowering sun still warmed the building there and glinted off its wavy panes of window glass. "It will be dark in another hour, and I don't see any good reason to spend one more night on hard ground when right up the street a ways is a place that lets rooms for two bits."

McGee glanced at the sign, then cast an eye about the town. "Maybe you're right. It's just that folks appear so jittery. And jittery folks makes me jittery, you know. I've a troubling feeling about this place, Cap."

McGee had a way of sniffing out trouble before it arrived, and if I'd been half as smart as I'd like to give myself credit, we'd have put Calico Lace far behind us. But we didn't.

I peered over the curve of my saddle at the saloon. It was two stories high, built of logs and rough-milled boards, with a steep tin roof for shedding heavy winter snows. From inside came the rattle of a piano. When I looked back, McGee was frowning.

"Let's get that drink. We'll be careful to mind our own business and turn in early tonight," I said.

McGee shelved his concerns and put on a grin. Where whiskey was concerned, McGee was not easily put off. We climbed to that tall sidewalk and pushed apart the batwing doors. The cool darkness inside was soothing to our sun-weary eyes. The low rumble of sociable conversation subsided as we crossed a creaking floor and took chairs at a table near the end of the long room. The piano missed a note as the man behind the keys craned his neck. Slowly the hum resumed.

It took some seconds for my eyes to adjust to the dim interior. When they did, I noted that the saloon was a long, narrow place with a dozen or so tables scattered about and a long bar stretching partway along one wall. The tables were mostly empty. I counted seven men, including the curious gent behind the ivories, and a scowling, hawk-nosed fellow in a dingy white apron. The piano stood opposite the bar, near the foot of a staircase that crawled up the wall to a dark second floor. Overhead hung two wooden chandeliers decked out with eight lamps each. A rope and pulley lowered them for lighting when the time came, and judging from the toothy shadows outside, that time was near at hand.

"Your regular, Cap?" McGee asked, offering to fetch the drinks.

I tossed McGee a coin and he trotted to the bar. The hawk-nosed gent behind the counter kept casting his scowl in my direction as he pulled out a bottle and took McGee's money. Most everyone in the saloon was stealing glances as if they were afraid to be too obvious about it. Their mumbling remained low, guarded, and I was beginning to wonder if I didn't have a hole in my britches somewhere, or maybe they figured my hat was stolen . . . or something.

McGee came back and set the bottle and two glasses on the table, frowning as he lowered into the chair and leaned close to whisper, "Ever get that feeling like you was walking across someone's grave, Cap?"

A chair scuffed back and a tall fellow under a wide, flat-brimmed hat got up and walked toward the door, his boots thumping heavy on the floor, rowels jingling. He stepped outside into the fading sunlight and peered at our horses tied there. With a final worried glance back over his shoulder, he stepped down off the sidewalk and angled across the street. I watched until he'd moved out of sight. McGee was studying me with his lips scrunched into a knot as he sometimes does when he is troubled about something.

"More like we are the ghosts from out of someone's grave," I replied, reaching for the bottle.

McGee grunted and I filled our glasses. "Let's wash down the trail dust and find us a room somewhere. Tomorrow we'll start early for Fountain Colony. I figure folks there aren't as nervous over strangers as they are here in Calico Lace."

McGee raised his glass. "I'll drink to that!"

McGee would drink to a toothache if nothing more promising offered itself.

"And to General Palmer and the railroad he's building," he added after a long lip-smacking pull at his glass. "Just hope he ain't yet gone and hired up all the surveyors he needs."

"To General Palmer." We drained our glasses and McGee refilled them again.

Their guarded stares and low talk chafed at me like an overstarched shirt, but the whiskey took the edge off our nerves, and so long as no one bothered us, we were in no hurry to leave. A half hour later the sun had reddened the sky to the color of blood and the barkeep was busy lowering the chandeliers and lighting the lamps. Men began to drift in off the streets. Calico Lace, it appeared, sat on the edge of two worlds. To the east lay the kingdoms of the cattle ranchers, in the foothills and the flat prairies that stretched clear back to Missouri, while to the west were the new mines. Gold had been discovered up north along Cherry Creek back in '59, and gold and silver camps had been spreading throughout these Rocky Mountains ever since. Calico Lace had been smartly placed to serve both industries.

Big hats, little hats. Chaps and overalls covered in rock dust. Work boots, riding boots. The men came boisterously through the batwings with drink and entertainment on their minds, but the quiet disease that had infected the saloon spread quickly.

McGee drained his glass and said, "How 'bout one more to top off the evening, Cap? I ain't going to have no trouble sleeping tonight, not with a real bed under me and all this civilized booze warming my belly."

I would have said no, but McGee splashed some more whiskey into our glasses without waiting. He set the bottle on the table with a thump and said, "How far you figure it is to Fountain Colony, Cap?"

Past McGee's shoulder I watched a man join up with three others who had begun to arrive a few minutes earlier. They were gathering up on the sidewalk outside, each taking a turn to look in at the crowded saloon. But it wasn't the smoky barroom that had their interests. Now they came through the batwings and moved along the wall. An uneasy electricity filled the air. I grimaced and looked back at McGee.

"Sixty . . . seventy miles yet, I reckon. Maybe two days of hard riding." Lamplight flashed off the amber whiskey in my glass. I drained it and leaned back to study the wall behind us. Heavy logs; solid as any Confederate redoubt McGee and I had faced at Port Hudson in '63. Not even a window. The staircase up to the second floor was the only way out of the saloon, and there was no telling what was up there.

McGee caught my worry. His blue eyes narrowed to hard lines and he said, "You're actin' a mite peculiar, Cap. Something wrong?"

"When was the last time we had to fight our way out of a boxed-in saloon?" I set the glass down, looking for another way. There was a door in the corner, near the long bar, but it was closed and bolted.

McGee thought for a moment. "Don't believe we ever had to do that," he said finally.

"There is a first time for everything," I noted grimly. "There is no way out of here except through those batwings. And there are men waiting out there. A few minutes ago four men came in, over there." I gave a small nod. McGee's view went to the wall. "Since then maybe a dozen more men have come in, but only three bothered to buy drinks. That tells me they have something else on their minds, and since it's you and me who seem to be the center of attraction, I have a feeling we are that *something else*."

McGee leaned closer and whispered, "You sure we ain't never been to this here Calico Lace afore?"

I grimaced. "Not as certain as I was half an hour ago."

"What are we going to do, Cap?"

It always came down to that. What are *we* going to do. Nearly a dozen civilian years separated us from that life that was the army, yet through all that time and all those long miles McGee still turned to me to make the decisions. To McGee I was still, and would forever remain, *Cap*. No matter how I tried to shake it off, it was one last responsibility I could not ride away from.

More men were gathering in the evening shadows, looking in over the top of the doors. Logistically speaking, they had us boxed in real tight. I never much cared for logic. It always seemed to get in the way when quick thinking was needed.

"If it is us they want, there is not much we can do about it now. If not, then we have worked ourselves up a lather over nothing. Either way, I don't much feel like having another drink."

"Maybe we can reach our horses and rifles," he said, pushing away his half-full glass.

I shook my head. "No rifles. I'm not so fond of Calico Lace that I care to spend eternity planted here, or staring at it from behind jail bars. If it's a fight they want, then that's what we will give them. Afterward, we can climb back on our animals and leave. If not, we'll thank the Fates, find us a room for the night, and be on our way come sunup."

"But why would they want to pick a fight with us?" McGee's eyes widened and shifted around the crowded room. "We ain't never been here—have we?"

I shrugged. McGee frowned then grabbed up his whiskey and gulped it down. The low murmuring fell silent when we scuffed back our chairs and stood. Halfway to the doors, I thought we just might make it. Then they came—and I realized that getting out of there was going to come at a price.

One glance and I knew these men; knew what they were and what they were not. They weren't your usual barroom bullies out to bust some heads. They were regular folk—store clerks, street muckers, stock handlers, cowboys, and rock moles from the local mines. And none of them looked very happy at the moment. The barber was among them. They came in through the batwings to block our way. The four along the wall moved across the floor then. Two were in shirtsleeves, a third wore the long jacket of a banker or lawyer. The fourth, taller and broader than his friends, wore a dusty brown corduroy vest and wide hat that kept the lamplight from showing me his eyes. Except for this one, they were all unarmed. Well, so were we.

McGee cast a worried look at me and said out of the corner of his mouth, "I'll just bet we've been here afore, Cap."

I was beginning to wonder too.

2

GAWKERS SCRAMBLED OUT of the way while the piano player forgot what he was being paid to do and joined the line forming up along the wall and up the staircase. The show was about to start. I gave a wry grin.

In the brief seconds as men made room, a chest-squeezing silence filled the room. Ruefully, I confirmed my first impression. McGee and I had been backed into a hole. Escape through the door was cut off, and the staircase was bunched up with wide-eyed spectators. Sloppy form, I mused, for a supposed hero of the first battle of Bull Run. Well, that had been a lot of years ago. A man is entitled to forget, or at least pack those old memories away where he doesn't have to come face-to-face with them every day of his life.

I pegged the man with the wide hat for a cow pusher. He stepped forward now, staying just beyond my reach, which was longer than most men's. He was tall and our eyes met level. His shoulders were wide, but there was no telling how much of that was muscle, and how much just bulk from his longhandles, wool shirt, and vest. The light in there was poor, but I could tell his dark face had seen a lot of sun and was etched like a piece of old weathered wood. His hard eyes fixed upon mine and I couldn't afford to look away, to give him that satisfaction. I was aware of the nervous twitch in his right hand where it dropped low to his side, close to the battered grips of a revolver there.

It suddenly occurred to me that this man was afraid. Afraid of me. I wasn't wearing iron and neither was McGee, but yet he was fearful, and not just a little unhappy facing me down.

"You aren't wearing those fancy guns of yours, Carver," he said tightly. "I am surprised."

Carver?

McGee looked at me, confused.

"You were warned never to come back to this town," he went on. "That wasn't just friendly advice. We meant it, every word."

Those men still sitting scuffed back their chairs and pushed in along the wall. The barkeep was scurrying about like a beaver snatching breakables off the bar and shelves and hiding them down below, overlooking a few bottles, thinking mostly about his glassware and a big fishbowl filled with shelled peanuts.

McGee was shaking his head. It was suddenly clear to both of us that this fellow thought I was someone else.

I said, "Sure you got the right fellow, friend?"

McGee chuckled and had started to explain when the man cut him off.

"You stay out of this, you redheaded squirrel!"

McGee bunched his knuckles and hunched forward. I was hoping to talk our way out of this one, but that had been the wrong thing to say. My Irish friend wasn't very tall, but he was a scrapping bearcat once you riled him, and he was riling up real good now. I put out a hand to hold him back until I got this confusion straightened out.

"I'm not your friend, Carver. Never have been," the man growled.

Just then something swept past the corner of my eye. I wheeled aside in time to see the silver-tipped walking stick crack down on McGee's head, flattening his hat and slamming his teeth together. The stick snapped in two and sailed into the crowd. McGee went down like a sack of flour.

Any chance of talking had ended.

A lot of what I had learned during the war had been safely tucked away somewhere in a remote part of my brain where I didn't have to think about it day to day. But it's funny how some things come back to you when you're not expecting them. One lesson I'd learned long ago was that when retreat was no longer an option, carrying the attack was all that was left, and any hesitation was a sure road to defeat. I didn't know why that memory was so clear and prodding at me just then, but I'm not one to ignore gut feelings.

I turned back to the burly cowboy and buried my fist into his solid belly just as fast and hard as I was able. The air burst from his throat as he buckled in half, his face showing shock. What had he expected, I wondered, driving my knee up to meet his nose and sprawling him back into the arms of some of his friends.

Turning left, I spied the fellow still clutching the short end of his broken walking stick, looking stunned. He was a man who didn't know why he had done what he had, or even if he should have. I didn't give him time to work it out. Confused as he was, he still had savvy enough to swing what was left of it at me when I went for him. I ducked under it and ratcheted his head back with an uppercut to his jaw. The crack was nearly as loud as his stick breaking across McGee's head. He staggered backward, arms wide and flailing, and crashed into the bar, slumping to the floor with a flood of blood turning his chin and shirtfront red.

Hands grabbed me from behind. I swung around, throwing up my arms to block the punch I somehow knew would be coming. A short jab sent the barber backpedaling into a table that splintered under his weight and crashed to the floor.

The confusion doubled around me, but somehow I settled down, comfortable in the melee and in the way the fight was running. I thought fleetingly of other skir-mishes fought in other times and places. Old reflexes and battle training came back effortlessly and the years seemed to fall away.

A fist came out of nowhere and clipped me on the chin. It was a poor punch, thrown from an awkward angle by a gent who looked as if he ought to be behind a teller's window counting out money to old women rather than mixing it up in the middle of a barroom brawl. He sucked in his breath and looked about to explode when the tip of my boot connected with his groin. Putting aside any further thoughts of fighting, the man gave out a wail of pain and collapsed into a moaning, squirming knot on the floorboards at my feet.

Like I said, your local barroom bullies they were not.

Hands grabbed at my shirt, at my vest, tore the hat from my head. I twisted free of them and dashed through a breach in their ranks with half a dozen men in hot pursuit. As I backed up against the bar, my view leaped for a weapon of some kind. McGee was on the floor, still out cold. I could expect no help from that quarter.

Two came at me but stopped just short of my reach, eyeing the hard knuckles that waited, beckoning them closer. Another man tore a twisted leg from a shattered table and waved it menacingly as he stalked forward. The whole place wanted in on the fight, wanted to get a piece of me. My fingers touched something on the bar and wrapped about the neck of a whiskey bottle overlooked in the rush to get things put away. I slammed it down on the edge of the bar and brought the broken glass to bear.

The two men closest to me instantly reconsidered and moved back a couple steps. The gent waving the table leg hesitated, glanced at the bodies already cluttering the floor, then at the jagged glass in my fist. It was a standoff while they all stood there wondering just how much they really wanted me, and how much they were willing to pay for the privilege. I got weary of waving the bottle at them and was about to get back to business. I was in the mood now to finish this out and didn't want it to end just yet. Then a voice rang out over the crowd, ordering us to break it up.

A wiry, gray-haired gent was pushing his way

through the crowd, the badge on his shirt glinting dully in the smoky light, the short double-barreled scattergun in his fists even duller. He stopped in front of me, a big-chested man with a scowling face beneath a tattered hat. He shot a glance at the gent fanning the air with his stick.

"I said break it up!" he barked. "Albert, drop that thing."

The man hesitated, then lowered the table leg and tossed it to the floor. From the looks of it, I figured Albert was as relieved to see this sheriff as I was.

The lawman's view swept over the skirmish, at the bodies scattered around, then turned the scattergun on me. "You too, Carver. Put that bottle down."

There it was again. I had never heard the name before but suddenly everyone was anxious to peg it on me. I let the bottle go and said, "Sheriff, I . . ."

"Shut up! I don't care to hear anything you have to say. I thought we were shed of you last winter, but here you turn up again. I swear, Carver, you are about as persistent as a bout of malaria. You just can't go away and leave us alone, can you?"

This mix-up had gone on too long, with no one the least interested in hearing what I had to say. McGee groaned. I looked at him, then across to the gun-totting sheriff. "Can I give my friend a hand?"

He nodded his gray head. "Go to him." The scatter-gun followed me.

Lifting McGee into a chair was about as easy as dragging a bag of wet sand. He groaned again and cradled his head in his hands, then opened his eyes and looked around.

"What happened, Cap?"

"Your thick skull went and busted someone's fancy walking stick."

He worked at focusing on me, then looked at the shattered tables, and the men being helped to their feet—those men able to stand. At least one unlucky gent was being carried off. I reckoned by tomorrow the local sawbones would have his jaw wired up tight and he'd be taking his dinner through a straw for a while.

McGee managed a crooked smile. "I see they finally ruffled your feathers to where you couldn't stand it no more, Cap. Sorry I missed it."

"You didn't miss much. Sheriff here broke it up just as it was getting interesting."

"Sheriff?" McGee noticed the old man with the scattergun then. "Mister, am I pleased to see you. Seems as folks around her has got the Cap here pegged fer some fellow named—"

A disturbance somewhere in the crowd cut him off. A worried-looking girl with long, strawberry-blond hair tied back with a yellow ribbon had just come through the batwings and was forcing her way past the men standing around us. She gave me one look and rushed with open arms, flinging them around my neck.

"Johnny, Johnny. My darling, are you all right? They didn't hurt you, did they?"

Before I could answer, her soft, yielding lips pressed against mine and her strong arms pulled us tight together. It happened so quickly it caught me off guard. She was a right pretty girl with eager lips, and it had been a mighty long time since a good-looking girl had kissed me that urgently. It lasted all of three or four seconds, though it seemed to me a lot longer than that, and I was just settling down enough to enjoy her lips when suddenly she pushed herself away and glared into my face.

"Who are you?" she gasped, her hand leaping protectively to her throat. She took a breath and scrubbed her lips with the back of her hand. "Who are you?" she demanded again, eyes wide and confused, flashing around at the smirking faces of the men standing there. The light in the saloon had been poor and I reckoned it might be easy to make such a mistake, but it hadn't taken her long to discover the error. And even in the miserable light it was plain that her fair skin was reddening up like a boiled lobster.

McGee was chuckling. "That's what we have been trying to tell you boys all along. I don't know who this Carver fellow is you keep mentioning, but this here is Captain Jacob Kellogg . . . retired."

Retired, hell, I thought I'd flat up and quit. But I didn't mention it right then. The woman's confused eyes searched my face. They were pale blue, complimenting her skin and hair in a most pleasing manner. She stepped back, hesitantly, as if still not certain, then looked at the grinning faces around her. Some of them had begun to laugh, enjoying her embarrassment almost as much as they had the fight. Well, there is no accounting for how some men take their entertainment. Then she lowered her beet-red cheeks, gathered up her skirts, and hurried out the door. I felt sorry for her, but there wasn't anything I could do to ease her humiliation.

The sheriff narrowed an eye at me, studying me for a spell. "You *aren't* John Carver?"

"Tried to mention it but no one gave me a chance."

He went on studying my face, still suspicious, then shook his head. "If you aren't, you must be his twin, Captain Kellogg." He glanced out over the crowd. "John Carver never had no twin brother, did he?" As far as anyone knew, he didn't. The sheriff frowned then turned to the man who had started the trouble. The cowboy was sitting in a chair, holding a towel to his bloodied nose. "Matt, reckon you owe this gentleman an apology . . . Reckon we all owe you an apology."

Matt shook his head. "I ain't convinced, Thad. No two men look so alike. If he ain't Carver I'll say the words, but first I need proof."

"You heard Julie. Who better would know than that girl?"

"Julie is his girl. She might be covering for him."

The sheriff reared back and gave the cowboy a skeptical look. Even he could see that Matt was stalling, not wanting to admit the mistake in front of all these men.

"Who is this man, John Carver, anyway?" I demanded. It was me, or at least my face, that had started this ruckus, and I figured I had more than just a passing interest in the matter.

The sheriff and the cowboy looked over as if they had forgotten I was there. Thad pursed his lips thoughtfully and began, "Why, John Carver is—"

But Matt cut him off. "Carver has an old bullet scar on his right arm, about three inches above the elbow." His voice held a challenge, and it got my neck hairs to bristling. I knew what he wanted. I was supposed to roll up my sleeve now and prove to them that I was who I claimed to be. Another time, I might have pushed the challenge right back at him, held my ground just for the principle of the thing, but not tonight. The ride down from Glenwood Springs had been long and tiring and right then I'd have shown him both arms if it meant getting a good night's sleep around here.

He was waiting, and so was the sheriff and everyone else. Their curiosity was piqued. Maybe Julie really was throwing up a hedge to protect her beau.

I rolled up the sleeve. A smile spread the sheriff's thin lips. "I knew Julie wasn't covering for him. She ain't that good a liar!"

Matt looked real disappointed. Finding a scar would have vindicated him. But he was a man of his word. The mistake had cost him a broken nose and a bit of pride, and all in all, I figured he'd gotten off cheap. I was willing to drop the whole matter.

"I apologize, mister. When you and your friend came into town a bunch of us just assumed ... Hell, like Thad said, you could be Carver's twin. I'm sorry we jumped the gun on you." He offered his hand and I took it. He had a strong grip, the grip of an honest man. "I'm afraid I didn't catch the name."

"Kellogg. Jacob Kellogg."

"Your friend called you 'Captain.' "

"That's just something left over from the war. McGee still prefers to use it, but that was a lot of years ago. Jacob Kellogg will do."

It was an awkward moment for him, and me. "Can I buy you and your friend a drink, Mr. Kellogg? I know it doesn't make up for what we did here tonight."

McGee's eye's brightened. I said, "I'll drink with you, but first you owe McGee an apology too."

"Naw, Cap. That ain't necessary."

"Yes, it is," Matt answered. "Sometimes I'm too free with my words, Mr. McGee. Oftentimes they come back and I regret them. I didn't mean anything by that remark 'bout the color of your hair. Why, my very own sainted mother had the fieriest hair you ever did see."

"No more said!" McGee stood and let out a moan, clamping a hand to his forehead. "Feels like I walked into a low doorway."

"Let's try to fix that up, Mr. McGee," Matt said to the aproned man removing his glassware from hiding, arranging it on the shelves in front of a long mirror etched with the figure of a woman reposed upon a cloud. "Millford. A bottle of your best, and four glasses." He glanced at the sheriff. "You will join us, Thad?"

Thad shook his head. "Thanks, but not right now. I was in the middle of supper when word came there was trouble brewing here. Millie will be waiting on me. Told her I'd be home soon as I could. Maybe later if I can get away. Nice meeting you, Mr. Kellogg, Mr. McGee. Regret the misunderstanding."

The crowd had begun to break up when Thad left. A man was hauling the shattered tables out through the back door, which had been unbolted and now stood open to the night. We found an empty table. Millford brought over a bottle and four glasses. Matt filled three of them and McGee instantly put the incident out of mind, washing down the last memories of the fight with a fast swig, reaching to refill his empty glass.

The mood in the saloon had changed. Talk was freer and louder. The piano music sounded more friendly too—at least that was the impression I had, sitting there nursing the whiskey in my glass. I leaned back in my chair, trying to assess the place in the light of its more friendly face. I still wasn't very fond of it, and doubted the feeling would be any different come morning.

But I had learned one thing for sure.

I knew for certain that McGee and I had never been in Calico Lace before.

3

MATT STRINGER WAS built like a quarry-stone roundhouse; a solid man with a leathered face that had seen too many summer suns, and a shock of stiff, graying hair not content to stay bound up inside his hat. He was a man of easy manners once he was relaxed, and after a couple drinks, Stringer was doing a fair job of relaxing. His nose had stopped bleeding, but he kept the bloody towel handy and dabbed at the swollen protuberance every so often just to make sure.

"Third time I busted up this nose," he allowed at one point. "Someday I will lose it permanent if I'm not careful."

McGee rubbed the lump that had sprouted atop his head. "And I best watch out for walking sticks in the future."

I grinned. The whiskey was making me easy too. "You could bust a singletree over McGee's head without causing too much damage—except maybe to the singletree."

They laughed and McGee pretended I'd wounded his feelings. "Aw, Cap, no need to get spiteful on me, now."

Matt refilled the glasses. "I'm thinking we made our peaceful little town look mighty unfriendly to you gents, didn't we?"

"It did appear that way," I said, sipping the whiskey.

"What brings you two here to Calico Lace?"

It was a fair question, but I caught the underlying note of concern in his voice. McGee must have missed it for he kept grinning at the glass in his fingers, swaying a bit, his face florid with the whiskey. "We've come down from Glenwood Springs, on our way to Fountain Colony, south of here a ways. Calico Lace just happened to be someplace in between."

"Just passing through?" He seemed to relax some again. "Fountain Colony? Isn't that the new town they are building below Pikes Peak?"

"General Palmer is putting together a railroad for himself, and I figure he needs a town to go along with it."

"Railroad? You two work for the railroad?"

"Not exactly. Right now we don't work for anyone. We were hoping to hire on as surveyors. McGee and I have done a lot of surveying over the years. Worked on the transcontinental line after the war and have been surveying on and off ever since. Got all our equipment on a packhorse out front. Word has it, Palmer is planning an extension of his line south of Pueblo down to San Luis. We were hoping to get some steady work for a change."

"Surveyors?" Matt raised his eyebrows, surprised,

and considered something a moment. "I was just talking to my foreman about finding us someone who could shoot a fence line along our north boundary, where the Iron Ridge camp touches C-N land. It's an awful rugged stretch of mountainside. About fifteen miles of it. It's a job for men who know what they're doing. You two wouldn't be interested in taking on the job?"

From the little I knew about cow camps and cattle, I recalled that fences and open ranges did not mix well. It was what kept the ranchers and sodbusters scrapping at each other; the cause of more than one range war and much spilled blood. It was something I didn't want to get in the middle of. Taking sides in something like that was too much like making a commitment, and I'd been more than successful at avoiding real commitments since I buried Betty and the twins.

I studied the craggy face across the table. "I was under the impression that fences were strictly frowned upon most anyplace west of the Mississippi."

"Fences?" He was mystified at first, then all at once he understood and grinned, shaking his head. "No, no, no, that's not it at all, Mr. Kellogg. I'm not planning to throw a wire along that stretch of land. I just want the boundary line staked out is all, so I know where the damned thing lays. Why, if I tried to build a fence across that hunk of real estate I'd have old Cliff Nelson breathing down my backside faster than corn through a chicken."

It was the sort of offer McGee and I had taken a hundred times. We'd worked our way across the West and back on small surveying jobs, and had it been another place or time I might have taken him up on it, but Calico Lace had left a bitter taste; one only a fresh mount and many miles was going to wash away. A man started for the door, then turned back and stopped by our table.

"Just wanted to tell you how sorry we all are for what happened, Mr. Kellogg," he said. I thanked him and he left. Folks here seemed friendly enough now, and maybe Calico Lace shouldn't have turned me sour. But I was no more fond of the place after he left. Matt Stringer must have been reading my thoughts.

"You know, first impressions aren't always the right ones."

I grimaced. "Thanks. But I think McGee and I will pass on your offer just the same." A glance told me that my Irish friend was more interested in his whiskey than the job I had just turned down. I should have known better than to worry about what McGee thought. He was all the time as agreeable as sin.

"Suit yourself. I can't say as I really blame you. We were a mite hard on you tonight." Stringer leaned back in his chair, dark eyes fixed upon my face. Stringer had a way of making the most innocent words ring loud with challenge. I ignored it. I wouldn't be badgered into something I didn't want to take on. Maybe it was because of that stubbornness that McGee and I had been drifting from place to place since the war's end. Whenever something came up that I didn't like, we would saddle up and leave.

The army had spent a lot of time and money on me trying to get those tried and true and honorable notions of discipline, responsibility, and leadership through my obstinate skull. My old commander, Colonel Harrison, would be hard-pressed to find any of those virtues left in his protégé, one ex-captain Jacob Kellogg.

But that line of thinking never did any good. I'd chased it around for years; chased, caught, buried, and resurrected and chased some more. Just then the sheriff stepped into the saloon and angled toward our table. It gave me an excuse to pack away those thoughts again.

"Looks to me like you three have patched up your differences."

Matt shoved back a chair. "Have a sit," he said and made the introductions proper. The sheriff's full name was Thaddeus Griever. He was a tall, wiry fellow with broad but bony shoulders that at one time in his distant youth had carried considerable muscle. But that was a long time ago, and now he looked tired, and a little frail, and I wondered what a man like him was doing still wearing a badge and carrying a gun. Creases deepened in his face and the backs of his nut-brown hands. His vest was faded and sagged some from his shoulders. The star pinned there looked as old as Griever himself, with nickel plating worn away in places, showing yellow along the edges where the brass lay exposed.

Griever gave us a thin smile as he settled in the chair. He'd left the scattergun at home, but a short-barrel Army Colt resided in a scuffed holster high on the back side of his narrow hips.

Matt filled the fourth glass and said, "I see Millie let you out for the evening."

Griever moved the glass in front of him and frowned. "Work, Matt. Always work," he lamented. "Someday these tired old bones of mine are going to get a rest, but that won't be until I retire."

"Not you, Thad. You'll never retire. You like work too much. Besides, the town council won't let you go."

He laughed. "Least not without a fight." He turned the glass on the tabletop, peering at it.

"Those old bones of yours won't find the rest they deserve till they're fast asleep under six feet of cold ground."

Griever gave a snort and said, "You're probably right, Matt." He turned his view on me—sharp, penetrating eyes they were; the eyes of a much younger man, but full of wisdom, and I knew right then that this was a man who had lived his life at a full gallop. He looked me over and shook his head. "Can't get over how much you look like him. Sure you ain't kin?"

I laughed. "Reckon that all depends on how far back you want to go."

Both he and Matt grinned. Thad said, "Anything before your granddaddy I can overlook." He glanced at McGee. "So, you and Mr. Kellogg served together during the war?"

"Aye. That we did. I was his first sergeant, I was," he slurred. "Fought side by side, we did. Fought for the glories of the North and Abraham Lincoln."

I nudged McGee under the table with my boot, but he was too drunk to notice. Griever cleared his throat, his expression hardening ever so slightly.

"Is that so?" Griever said evenly. "I never had the privilege of serving, but I have a son who spent some time in uniform."

"Did he really, now? And whereabouts was his out-fit?" McGee asked. Drunk as he was getting, McGee did a horrible job of hiding the suspicions that came with his words.

"That war was a lot of years ago," I broke in. "Too far back to start bringing it up now." Most people didn't care to reminisce about those years, and it made no difference what side they fought on. But McGee took particular delight in recounting the tales. It was a time when every man was your brother . . . in spirit, at least. For McGee, who had no family, it was a particularly fond period in his memory. I was hoping to get us off that track, for whenever McGee got wound up reliving past glories, it usually ended up unwinding in a brawl. And I wasn't prepared to fight another war tonight.

Neither, apparently, was the sheriff. "I totally agree with you, Mr. Kellogg. The past is past and I suggest we leave it there—buried, but not forgotten." He paused and stared at McGee. "Just like those fine, brave boys . . . of the Confederacy."

A heaviness settled over the table. McGee slid me a look that I'd seen a time or two. Right then I knew it could go either way. Griever saw it too. There was little I could do to stop him if he took it in his head to take offense to the sheriff's words. Like I said, McGee hauled around some pretty strong feelings about those days.

I laughed to break the tension. "You had that com-ing, McGee," I said and that was about all I could do.

McGee screwed up his lips and thought it over some. The moment passed and I knew we'd avoided another war when he raised his glass to the old man and said, "I sometimes run off at the mouth, Sheriff. Cap, here, he has got himself a full-time job on his hands just keeping me out of trouble. Reckon I can't go on fighting you Johnny Rebs the rest of my natural days, now can I? My apologies."

Griever smiled as if he'd known all along how this was going to end. "Forget it, son" was all he said.

Stringer had kept quiet all this time, watching with a certain detached curiosity. There'd been a devilish glint in his eyes as McGee and Griever tested each other. Now that the confrontation was over, he said, "Two things you don't want to discuss with Thad. Railroads are one of them, and you just found out what the other was."

"Railroads?" I said, surprised.

Stringer grinned, but I could see it was a warning of sorts.

Griever was grinning too. He finally picked his glass off the table and peered at the amber light coming through it from the lamps overhead. "You don't want to know, Mr. Kellogg. You just don't want to get me started on that one." He saluted me with the glass and said, "To your health, Mr. Kellogg, Mr. McGee."

We drank to health and prosperity. That devilish glint was still in Stringer's eyes, and I figured we had picked us a powderkeg of a town to light upon. One with a short fuse, and no matter how I tried to avoid it, it seemed I kept striking matches.

4

"JOHN CARVER?" GRIEVER repeated the name slowly, turning it into a question each time. "I swear if you aren't the spitting image," he noted again and I was getting weary of hearing it. "I only hope you haven't got that man's temper. Since you aren't wearing iron, I take it you can't use a six-shooter like he can . . ."

McGee opened his mouth to dispute that. I managed to get his attention this time with my boot and he stopped himself, refashioning the protest into a fake cough and quickly dousing it with another long swallow of Matt's whiskey. The bottle was below the halfway mark and my red-faced friend had accounted for most of the damage. He'd have a hard time of it in the morning, but I was determined to push on to Fountain Colony in spite of the hangover he was setting himself up for.

After McGee's run-in with Griever over the Lincoln-Davis disagreement of a dozen years ago, I wanted to change the subject, directing it onto more neutral ground. Since there wasn't much unusual in the weather, or the time of day, I had brought up the only curiosity left; a certain gent named John Carver, who, through some quirk in breeding, apparently resembled me in a striking way. I thought it would be safe ground now, and that was when Griever had turned his gaze back on me like seeing a ghost and began reciting the man's name.

". . . but from what I saw tonight, you'd be a fair match with your fists. Maybe better. That is all right by me. If two got a disagreement and settle it with their fists, I have no problem with that. I'll stand back and let them have at it, and maybe even wage a dollar or two on the strongest and wiliest between 'em. But when they reach for guns . . . or table legs or broken-off whiskey bottles, Mr. Kellogg"—his eyes narrowed a mite—"well, that's when I step in and put a stop to it. That's my job.

"Now, you take a man like John Carver. He has this love for guns; real fancy guns. He wears two of 'em, though I can't for the life of me understand why. Hell, one is heavy enough, even worn up high on the belt so as it don't flop again' your leg all the day long. But two?" Griever shook his head. "It must be for showing off to the ladies, or the man has a real uncertainty about himself to put up with that kind of punishment."

Griever tasted his whiskey, dainty like, with his little finger stuck out. In the time he'd been there he had lowered the level in his glass only by a scant cat's whisker. "Carver wears his guns low, like Matt, here. But he ties them down real tight." He gave a short laugh. "One day them pins of his are going to wither up and fall off."

Matt snickered.

McGee grinned and groped for the bottle to refill his glass—again.

"Pretty guns they are too. Nickel-plated and engraved all over. The grips are of ivory and the actions honed down slick as pond ice. And one more thing, Mr. Kellogg. That man is good, real good, best I have ever seen. Used to spend hours practicing with them. Didn't have much of anything else to do. No one would hire him on for decent work after what he had done at Mary's place. Unreliable." Griever shook his head. "Some men are just like that. Carver wasn't good for anything but shooting up whiskey bottles out behind Hiram's Livery . . . and tending the horses there. Had a way with horses." He gave a short laugh. "Reckon everyone has their gift. But with some men you just have to look harder to find it."

The story lapsed and Griever shook his head, remembering. "Fancy guns all right, but I wouldn't own them, not if he was to give 'em to me all wrapped up in fancy birthday paper."

"Why is that?" I asked.

"They'd be of no use to me. The action was honed too light. Liable to go off accidental and shoot my big toe or something. And all that nickel plating—looks pretty if all you're doing is wearing it for show. But a working gun? No sir. They'd flash like a mirror in the sunlight. Give away your position; get you killed, they would. I suppose they'd be all right for cowboying. Cows don't much pay attention to such things and nickel won't rust when it up and rains on you. But for police work? Nope, I wouldn't own 'em."

Thad Griever was a man of deep opinions, and I was curious about his grudge against the railroad. But I didn't want to ask right then. The old man spoke with a certain graveness tempering his words. Matt sat quietly, listening, the line of his jaw rigid, as if his face were chiseled from a block of dark granite. I caught the feeling that whatever had happened here in Calico Lace, it wasn't a thing he felt comfortable recalling. I finished the whiskey in my glass and turned it over. I'd had enough.

Griever picked up the thread of his story. "It was about two years ago that John Carver first cast his shadow over Calico Lace. He came down from the north, like you two, riding a leggy sorrel. We didn't pay him much mind, as he looked like any other drifter come out of the mountains. Maybe he was looking for work in the mines to the west of us, or on his way east to punch cows out Castle Rock way. We get drifters through here time to time. Most don't stay long. But this one did. He must have been short on money 'cause he started looking for work right off. Carver seemed friendly enough, so it wasn't long before he snagged himself steady employment.

"Filby hired him on to tend the boiler out behind his bathhouse. Carver toiled at keeping those iron pots bubbling for a week or two. But that job ended right quick one morning when the hot water ran out and Filby found his new employee drunk as an Indian back behind the wood stack. Ernie Filby is a preacher's kid, you see. His pa was a circuit rider and drummed this fool notion into his head that drink was sin."

Griever shook his head and gave a wry smile. "Don't know where them religious folk get that notion. I'm not a churchgoing man, but I have read the Good Book. I seem to recall the Lord went and miracled himself up a couple barrels of wine for this here party they was throwing." He grinned. "But I'm getting off the track. Do that from time to time. We was talking about Carver."

Griever seemed an easygoing fellow, and not afraid to speak his mind. I liked that in a man. I glanced at McGee. Drink *was* getting the best of him. He clutched his glass hard against the table as if it wanted to run away, and his eyes were glazing over, staring unblinking out across the smoky barroom. I don't think he was tracking Griever's story very closely. His sodden eyes shifted toward me and his mouth twisted up into a grin. At least he was still conscious. He hiked the glass to his lips and drink sloshed over its rim. McGee was following an old and familiar pattern. It wouldn't be long now before he burst out into song; something Irish, and with it the thick brogue he managed to cover over when he was sober.

"After Filby gave him the boot, Carver went back to knocking on doors, finally landing on Mary's front step. Mary Kenyon is a kindly woman who runs the local hash house. Her heart went out to the bum, and before you knew it, he was scrubbing dishes at her place." Griever paused, tobacco-yellowed teeth worrying his lower lip while his bright eyes clouded over. "I suppose that was the start of all the trouble," he said thoughtfully. "You see, Mary has a gal working for her who is about the prettiest filly you ever did see—well, you *did* see her, Mr. Kellogg." He gave a short laugh. "Julie Albright. She slings hash at Mary's eatery. A man would have to be bat-blind not to take notice to Julie. Now, John Carver has more than his fair share of bad qualities, but being bat-blind ain't one of 'em.

"And neither is Julie," he went on after a moment. "That surprised me. For a gal with so many young roosters strutting for her attentions, she actually took a fancy to Carver. The two of 'em started seeing each other after working hours.

"Up to now the only thing we really knew about Carver was his affection for the bottle and for nickel-plated Colts. But after Julie came into the picture, we began to see another side of him."

Griever paused to finish his whiskey. I reached for the bottle, but he smacked a palm over the rim and shook his head. "Still on duty. A man needs to know his limits. Say, you fellows getting tired of hearing all this nonsense?"

"Saints preserve us, no!" McGee exclaimed before I could answer. You can always tell when McGee has had too much to drink. He is as American as an ornery army mule; born and raised in New York City. But his parents were Irish immigrants and reared their son speaking the brogue. He keeps it pretty much under control when he is sober. But drunk, there is no telling what might come out of his lips. "Ye be getting to the best part," McGee slurred. I was amazed he'd kept up with the story this far.

"Well, if I'm gonna keep jawing, I'm gonna need me a glass of water."

"I'll get it, Thad," Stringer said, kicking back his chair. He moved stiffly to the bar, and I had the impression he'd just been looking for an excuse to stand and stretch his legs. Mine were cramping too. I shoved them out under the table and rocked back in the chair. McGee tried to refill his own glass. Griever watched him with a tight grin cut into his face. When Matt returned, Griever took a long drink then smacked his lips. "Ah, that's better. Now, where was I."

"Carver meets Julie," I prompted.

"Oh, yes. Like I said, we began to see the other side of this fellow. Jealousy. It's a fearful trait, Mr. Kellogg, especially when you've got a temper atop it. Julie had herself a following at the time. Occasionally some young fellow would come visiting at Mary's hash house. By this time Carver had this notion that he owned exclusive rights on Julie. The first trouble happened out behind Mary's place. Carver beat young Paul Wilcocks nearly to death. He used only his hands, but Carver is a big man, like yourself—six-three, six-four.

"If it had been my business, I'd have fired the hothead right then and there. But like I said, Mary is a kindly lady. The next time it happened, Carver didn't even have the decency to take his temper out behind the building. He commenced to beating a fellow right in the middle of all the breakfast customers. It was some poor vagabond whose only sin was an eye for beauty and a few words spoken." Griever frowned. "He didn't make it through the night. I'd have run Carver out of town except, like with Wilcocks, he only used his fists, and the man was a big, strapping fellow who should have been better able to take care of himself.

Hell, I can't run men out of town because they get into fistfights!" He shook his head, and I got the feeling this was something he struggled with often. "But I should have," he said finally.

"It was more than Mary could abide and she gave Carver the boot right there on the spot. He moped around town for days, and I believe he would have gone on to greener pastures if it wasn't for Julie. They had themselves a real burning romance by this time, though I never did figure out what the gal ever saw in the man. Whatever it was; it kept her by his side."

Griever put the glass to his lips, saw that it was empty, and set it down, with a frown on his tired face. "Figuring that Carver couldn't get into too much trouble around horses, Hiram hired him on at the livery, shoveling manure and pitching hay." Griever grinned. "Hell, them animals were about the only critters could kick harder than him. Hiram reckoned Carver wouldn't be picking any fights with them, and like I said, he was real good around horses. The arrangement appeared to be working out fine. Things began to settle down . . . then the shooting began.

"First time I heard it I thought we had us a massacre in the works. I grabbed up my old scattergun and went hopping on down to the stables where the shots were coming from. I pulled up short at the corner of the barn and peeked around it. But it was only Carver, alone, busting a row of empty whiskey bottles lined out on the top rail of one of the corrals.

"I watched him awhile, not letting on I was there. Mighty impressive shooting. I'd think three . . . four times before calling his hand."

Griever grew introspective, his gaze fixed upon empty space, remembering. The past is like that. It has a way of coming back and grabbing hold of you in the most unlikely of places. Sometimes you try to hold onto those brief moments—if the memories are pleasant. Other times you flee from them like a nightmare. Mostly I've been running from mine. I wondered what Griever did with his. Matt shifted his weight. The creak of his chair brought Griever back to the present. He cleared his throat.

"That practicing went on for weeks and I had a bad feeling that real trouble was in the makings, back there behind the livery. It was about this time that young Joey Nelson comes into the story. Him and Julie had been friends for a good many years. Nothing serious the way I seen it, just friends. Joey lived out on the C-N and didn't make it into town much. When he did come down out of the mountains, him and Julie would get together. As it happened, the few times Joey was in Calico Lace, Carver wasn't . . . but not the last time."

Griever's eyes narrowed, remembering. "Those two locked horns like bucks in rutting season. Joey Nelson was big, and his papa, Cliff Nelson, had taught him that when pushed, you push back twice as hard. His sister, Penny, she's like that too. Joey must have been feeling indignant at this interloper putting his brand to Julie . . ." Griever paused a moment, wonderment coming to his eyes. "Now as I think back on it, maybe Joey did carry a torch for Julie. He just never let on like Carver did. Well, Carver had already staked his claim and wasn't about to be run off. If he couldn't whip

Joey with his fist, he could with his revolvers. He badgered him into a gunfight, and before I could stop it, it was all over. Nothing I could do to help. Poor Joey was facedown in the street spilling his life into the dust. Dust!" Griever growled angrily, wagging his gray head. "Dust," he repeated softly. "It is heartless stuff, Mr. Kellogg. It will suck you dry, then the wind scatters it to the four corners, leaving no trace where a man died. Heartless stuff this country is made of."

Stringer glanced away and pretended to study something at the bottom of his empty glass. McGee tried for the bottle, missed, and caught it on the way back. Our table grew silent while the sounds of the saloon grew distant and unreal and I pondered Griever's words. It *was* an unforgiving land; unforgiving and relentless; a place that rarely allowed more than one mistake . . . but then that description might also fit the safe and settled farmlands of Ohio, I decided bitterly, the past threatening to reach across the years to me now. I fought it down, suppressing those haunting memories I could never be truly free of. I'd had too much to drink, and that always made it harder to resist them.

Griever's voice rescued me from the ghosts of my past. "Doc Perry tried to save him." He shook his head and drew in a ragged breath. "According to witnesses, it had been a fair fight. Carver had badgered him into it all right, but Joey had drawn first.

"By this time folks had about had their fill of Mr. John Carver. A group of citizens got together to remedy the situation. It weren't exactly a legal committee, so I grabbed my fishing pole and rode into the mountains for a few days. Ain't saying I'm proud of what I done, but I'd do it again if need be. There is the letter of the law, and then there is what's right. This was the right thing. Anyway, I fully expected to find Carver planted when I got back, but Matt here and a few others had more sense than that. They ran Carver out of town. Put quite a scare into the fellow, or so I'm told. Carver is a fighter, but he ain't awful brave when his back is against a wall. Reckon that's why he feels the need to weigh himself down with all that iron. Anyway, he saw the prudence in leaving Calico Lace. That was last fall."

Griever's story left a question lingering in my brain. "Where did he go?"

The sheriff shrugged his shoulders. "Don't know for sure, but he ain't too far off."

Matt had held his tongue this whole time. He leaned forward in his chair, pressing his arm onto the table. "I heard he was working cattle over at Castle Rock."

"That might be," Griever allowed.

Reflecting on the story, I decided a man like Carver wouldn't just up and leave, not with Julie Albright still around. "If it was me, it would take a whole lot more than a bunch of angry townsfolk to keep me from a girl I cared about."

Griever pursed his lips, thinking it over some, and said, "It's like this, Mr. Kellogg. We know that Carver is coming by now and again to see Julie, but so far he has kept out of sight. And he ain't made any trouble. And so long as it stays that way, I'm not going to go out of my way looking for him. Folks here in Calico Lace would just as soon forget the fellow."

Griever pulled a watch from his vest pocket. "Good

Lord. Will you look at the time. Half past ten already. I've got to be on my way. Got rounds yet to make." He stood and looked at me. "It was a pleasure meeting you, Mr. Kellogg and Mr. McGee. You planning to stick around town awhile?"

"We'll be on our way to Fountain Colony in the morning, Sheriff."

"Well, have a good trip."

Griever tugged his hat down low and strode out the batwing doors. When he had gone, I shifted my view to McGee, who was nursing the last of his whiskey. "It's about time we find us a room somewhere."

"Here, here! I'll drink to that!" McGee slurred.

"You'd drink to a thunderstruck buffalo stampede. Let me give you a hand."

Matt Stringer said, "The Calico Lodge is the only decent place in town to get a room. I'll help you with your friend."

We hoisted McGee between us and guided him outside. The cool night air slapped McGee in the face and seemed to momentarily clear his head. He peered up at the stars in the clear mountain sky and declared, " 'Tis a grand time to be singin' a song!" He bellowed out a tune that sounded vaguely like "Irish Eyes," belting out the words in a slurred brogue loud enough to raise the local boneyard.

We helped him across the street, boot tips hoeing twin furrows in the dirt. McGee was into the second verse by the time we hauled him up the steps to the boardwalk and into the hotel. Inside the dimly lit building Matt disappeared through a door, coming back a few moments later with a foggy-eyed gent wearing a nightshirt and a cap perched sideways upon his balding head. He appeared confused, his sleep-laden eyes casting about as if searching for the source of some annoyance.

"A room for my friends," Stringer said.

I signed the register as the man scowled at McGee.

"Tell your friend to stop that caterwauling. He's going to wake all the guests."

"What guests, Carmichael?" Matt asked

The owner bristled and snatched a key from its hook. "Can't you keep him quiet? What's wrong with him, anyway?"

I grinned. "I'll see what I can do."

McGee gave the man a crooked smile, put a finger to his lips and shushed him. Me and Stringer hauled McGee up a flight of stairs and swung him onto one of the beds. He snorted, flopped an arm over the edge, and passed out.

Matt gave a small smirk. "He'll be hurting in the morning."

"Won't be the first time," I allowed.

Grinning, Matt said good-bye. I closed the door after him and opened a window to let the stale air out. Below, Matt stepped into a rectangle of pale light that spilled from the hotel's doorway into the street. He stood there, drew in a deep breath, then took the steps down to the street and crossed to his horse tied to the hitching rail next to our animals. He swung into his saddle, turned his horse away, and faded into the night.

I glanced back at our animals, then turned my eyes up the street. Hiram's Livery was at the far end. It was dark, though someone might be there yet.

Not quite as far down the street I spied a sign on one of the buildings, pale in the moonlight. I could just make out the words painted on it. "THE KENYON CAFÉ." Someplace for breakfast in the morning before we left. I pulled my head back into the room.

McGee was sawing wood when I quietly closed the door behind me. The lobby was empty. Outside in the chill air I studied the street again. No one was about, but light and voices were still spilling from the saloon's doorway. I took our animals up the street to the livery. No one was awake in the large barn. A door to a small room off to one side was closed. A caretaker was likely asleep there but I didn't wake him. I put the animals up myself.

5

I POKED MY head out the window the next morning, trying to recall the clear night skies of only a few hours ago. But now my view ended abruptly against a dense gray wall. The air was soggy, the street was soggy, the windowsill, I discovered upon withdrawing my damp hands, was soggy. The buildings across the street were enshrouded with gray, swirling clouds, heavy with moisture that stiffened the joints and chilled the bones. I closed the window with a wistful glance to the east. But the fog that had settled upon Calico Lace sometime during the night was too thick for even the faintest warming rays of sunlight to break through.

"Wonder what time it is."

"Who cares?" McGee croaked from under an arm folded across his eyes. He raked his dry lips with his tongue and gave a low groan as he rolled off his pillow and sat on the edge of the bed, cradling his head in his hands. His eyes were bloodred when he looked at me, apparently having trouble focusing. When he'd got it worked out, he looked past me out the window.

"What is that, Cap? Snow?"

"It's still August. You haven't been asleep that long." I snatched my watch from the dresser. "It's nine-thirty. Half the morning is gone."

He moaned and put his head gently back into the pillow. In a moment his fingers began examining the knot atop his skull.

"Hurt?"

"Like a boil needing lancing. A regular Pikes Peak!"

"You had yourself one too many walking sticks last night and not enough whiskey?"

McGee swiveled a crimson eye my way. "You ain't funny at all, Cap."

"Get up and we'll find us some breakfast." I pulled him by the arm. Groggily, he sat on the edge of the bed again. I said, "Took the horses down to the livery last night. They should be ready to carry us a good thirty miles before nightfall."

"Thirty miles?" McGee's eyebrows lifted, then fell back low over his inflamed peepers. He smacked his lips and brought up a finger to examine them. "Got me a pair of boots softer than these, Cap. Thirty miles . . . ? How 'bout we stay here another day and start out tomorrow? General Palmer ain't gonna get his whole railroad surveyed in one day anyway."

He slumped back to the pillow and squeezed his eyes shut. They popped open and looked at me. "Why you suppose Sheriff Griever don't like railroads? That's mighty peculiar if you ask me."

I pulled McGee back into a sit. "A lot of things seem

peculiar here. That's why we are leaving today. I'm not at all thrilled walking around town with a face some folks would relish throwing a fist at. You should have seen the hotel clerk last night giving me the evil eye. Get yourself ready. You'll feel better with some eggs and bacon, and a pot of black coffee, filling your belly."

McGee frowned then wobbled to his feet and staggered over to the mirror, where he made faces at himself then splashed some water onto his face. He tugged his hat upon his wiry red mane and said, "Point me in the direction of the nearest privy and I'll be ready as I'm ever going to be."

We gathered up our Winchesters and went down to the lobby. It was still empty this early in the day and we ventured out into the chilled air and found the privies out back. Then we made our way through the pea soup and across the street.

"Well, it sure do feel like winter," McGee groused as we plowed through the fog toward the Kenyon Café.

The place was practically empty. I wasn't surprised. By ten o'clock on a Tuesday morning most folks were off to work somewhere. Few wear the label of *no-account drifter* as well as McGee and me. Just as well. I wasn't anxious to run into anyone packing knuckles for the gent with the misfortune to look like me. We took a table by the wall.

A woman came through the swinging double doors from the steaming kitchen in back. She was tall, though not overly so. A narrow waist and bare tawny arms gave the impression of height, and her easy manner reminded me of a soap bubble floating across the floor.

Then she was standing by our table, peering curiously at me with wide, brown eyes, and I grinned back. Her hair was dark and long, tied back from her face with a light blue ribbon. And what a face. I was staring. Her radiant complexion seemed to glow from a fire deep within her very soul; a shining beacon, I thought just then, for such a gloomy and dismal morning as this. Her eyes sparkled, her smile was wide and friendly, and when she suddenly shook her head, a shower of hair cascaded across her shoulders.

"Julie was right. You *are* the very image! Oh, please forgive me, I didn't mean to stare."

"That's all right. I'm beginning to get used to it." I was staring too. With some effort I forced my eyes from her lovely face, wondering if I should stand and make with the introductions or keep sitting there with a stupid grin on my face.

Graciously, she pretended not to notice my dilemma. Her smile widened. "I'm Mary Kenyon. I heard all about that dreadful misunderstanding last night."

My view leaped again, recalling Sheriff Griever speaking of Mary Kenyon. Judging from his words, I had pictured Mary Kenyon an old spinster years past her prime. But this woman standing before me was far from that. If anything, she was just approaching it, I decided. I did not consider myself an old warhorse to be turned out to pasture at forty-one. And this stunning woman had to be at least five years shy of that mark.

"Word gets around fast."

"Julie works for me," she said, smiling. "I heard all about it soon as I got in this morning. It's Mr. Kellogg, isn't it? And Mr. McGee?"

McGee tried to smile. I told her I was pleased to make her acquaintance—and I was.

"What can I get you two gentlemen?"

We ordered a pile of eggs and all the fixings. Mary turned to leave then looked back, studying my face a moment. "What were you just staring at, Mr. Kellogg?"

My cheeks warmed, but there was no hiding my embarrassment. I had hoped my fascination had not been so obvious. But then, I had never been very good at hiding my feelings. "It was nothing, Mrs. Kenyon. It is just the way the sheriff described you to us last night. I . . . well, I expected Mary Kenyon to be a woman well on in years, that's all."

She laughed. "Thad Griever considers himself the patriarch of Calico Lace. I suspect he is only looking out for the well-being of the ladies of the town. I shall have to speak to that old coot." Smiling, she turned away, but stopped at the kitchen doors and turned back. "By the way, Mr. Kellogg, it is *Miss* Kenyon." Then the doors swung closed behind her.

McGee grinned at me. "Quite a looker, heh, Cap?"

"That she is, McGee, that she is."

"*Miss* Kenyon. Hear the way she said it? Sure you wouldn't want to spend a couple days here in Calico Lace after all?"

"I'm sure."

"She seemed pretty interested."

"I said I'm sure." But I wasn't one hundred percent. Life hadn't gotten me to the point where a pretty gal didn't still get my blood to rushing and my heart to thumping.

McGee shrugged. "I was just thinking of your own well-being, Cap, that's all."

"Sure you were. And anyway, the best thing for *my* well-being is to see Calico Lace over my shoulder from the back of my horse."

The coffee was prompt. Eggs and bacon, Mary informed us, would be forthcoming. I watched her shapely form recede through the kitchen doors once more with the swish of her skirts across the wooden floor.

Like McGee had said, she was quite a looker.

McGee shoved away his plate and leaned back in the chair, content as a cat on a lap. "Now that was a breakfast to set a man on his feet," he declared. "But I still ain't too anxious to climb back into the saddle, Cap."

Mary brought over a pot and refilled our cups, leaving us her pretty smile to contemplate as she went off to see to some customers who had just come in. Then a face framed in strawberry-blond hair peeked out from the kitchen doors. Hesitantly, Julie Albright came to our table. She was wearing a yellow dress beneath a dingy apron. Her watery blue eyes went well with the pale skin. Her lips showed a tinge of pink that, if not exactly natural, was discretely demure just the same. She couldn't have been more than eighteen or twenty, and I wondered how she had mistaken an obviously older critter like myself for her boyfriend. Well, the saloon had been poorly lit, and it was easy to be confused, what with the brawl and all, and men standing around. She did catch onto her mistake real quick once she planted that kiss, which I remember so well. I couldn't decide if that was good or bad.

"Hello. My name is Julie," she said uneasily.

"Yes, I know. We met last night," I replied glibly, trying to put her at ease.

Her cheeks flushed. Not such a great trick considering her pale complexion. She averted her eyes. "I wanted to apologize for that. It was bold and . . . and very unbecoming. I am sorry."

"I didn't mind, really. Fact is, I rather enjoyed it."

Her face grew redder. "You are not making this easy, Mr. Kellogg."

"Sorry. I don't mean to embarrass you. The fact is, you did McGee and me a big favor. If it wasn't for you, they might still think I was your boyfriend, and from what I understand, that's not the best way to keep healthy here in Calico Lace."

Julie's lips turned down. "They have Johnny figured all wrong, Mr. Kellogg. They just don't understand him. Oh, he has a temper, and is a bit jealous," a wistful smile touched her lips, "but that's just what they see on the surface. Inside he is a sweet man only looking for someone to understand him and take him for what he is."

I thought over the story Griever had told. Carver had killed two men out of jealousy, and beaten up a third. I wondered what could be *sweet* about a man like that? If folks had misjudged John Carver, maybe Julie was one of them. I considered my words and said, "I don't intend to judge him. All I have heard is one side of the story. Maybe you know another." One thing was for sure. I wasn't planning to stick around long enough to worry about the right or wrongness of people's opinions.

That seemed to satisfy her. "Well, I just wanted to say I was sorry for all the trouble you had, just because you look like Johnny." She paused and cocked her head to the right. "In the daylight, I can see the differences."

"Differences?" I hitched up a curious eyebrow.

"You are a little taller and older, and your eyes are the wrong color. His are soft brown and yours are gray."

I laughed. "I am certainly glad to hear that."

She smiled too. After Julie had gone back into the kitchen, McGee sat there grinning and shaking his head. "Finish up your coffee and let's get out of here," I said.

"I don't know what sort of love potion you got working for you, Cap. Whatever it is, it's working overtime at attracting good-looking women your way."

"What do you mean?"

"Well, first there was *Miss* Mary Kenyon who come over making eyes at you, then there was Julie—she's a smart-looking filly too. And while you was talkin' to her, I was watching a third handsome female giving you the once-over from the sidewalk outside the window. She is still standing there. If you don't turn too fast and spook her, you can catch a glimpse."

I gave McGee a wry smile and dropped my napkin. As I bent to retrieve it, I saw the tallish girl in a brown split skirt. She wore a matching jacket over a white blouse. The jacket looked a bit dusty, as if she had just ridden into town. A scarf covered her head, hiding the color of her hair. She gave a startled look when she discovered my ruse and hurriedly turned away.

McGee was chuckling.

"Let's get out of here," I said, finishing my coffee. "Pretty women are just dandy, but I'm used to handling them one at a time. I'm not interested in trying for any records. Not as young as I once was." Actually, I wasn't used to handling pretty women at all. I'd been a long time out of practice, and for the moment at least, that was the way I preferred it to stay.

The fog had begun to lift and a yellowish glow above the steeply sloped rooftops was reassuring. The sun was slowly winning out over the heavy clouds that still clung stubbornly to the ground.

"It's going to be a good day," McGee remarked as we started up the street toward Hiram's Livery.

I glanced at a patch of blue sky breaking through the fog. It gave me a warm feeling despite the chill that still put an edge to the air. I had to agree with McGee. It was shaping up to be a fine day.

Ahead, I saw the girl in the brown riding skirt step from a doorway and start our way. There was a certain determination to her steps and I had to wonder if McGee wasn't right. Pretty women seemed to be coming at me from out of the woodwork.

I determined to make the best of it, and as we drew closer, I gave her a smile and tried to think of something friendly to say; something that would get us on our way as quickly as possible without being impolite. But she didn't seem to notice my efforts. Her wide eyes were fixed upon me as her teeth clenched down in a rigid jaw. As she got closer, I noticed her left arm pressing the purse tight against her breasts. Her right hand was inside the purse, grabbing for something.

Then she withdrew her fist, and clutched tightly in it was a Colt's revolver. Her eyes were cold and locked unblinking upon my face. My breath caught in my throat and I froze there on the sidewalk, too stunned at first to move.

The girl's mouth began to move but I couldn't understand the words. McGee was shouting something at my side. His words were lost in my spinning brain. My attention was full upon the revolver in her hand.

She leveled the piece and I heard the hammer being dragged back; *click, click, click . . . click*. For a moment it was just the two of us, and we were frozen in time. Then her words reached out to me, empty of feeling, cold as the chilled air around me. It happened so fast I was only vaguely aware of McGee moving to my right.

"This is for Joey," she said.

Those were the last words I heard as she pulled the trigger.

6

*DEARLY BELOVED. WE are gathered here
in the sight of God to commend into His hands the souls
of . . .*

The words droned on, falling dully upon my ears
from a distance, far beyond the dark stand of ancient
oak trees, past a border of heavily scented lilac bushes.
As if by an invisible cord, the words pulled at me,
tugging me along, drawing me through the forest to the
very edge, where the violet wall stopped me. I dropped
to the soft earth and on hands and knees parted the
lower branches. Beyond was a black iron bar fence.
Mounds of black, black dirt marked each hole. Mourners, dressed in black, stood with shoulders slumped,
heads bent. A man in black, holding a black book, was
speaking while all around me gaily colored birds sang
their cheerful hearts out. The sweet odor of lilac was
too oppressive to bear so I crawled through the bushes,
through the iron bars, and stood at the man's side.

Ashes to ashes.

Dust to Dust.

Then it was suddenly very quiet. The mourners turned silently away and started out through the tall wrought iron cemetery gate where black coaches pulled by black horses waited.

"Who died?" I asked quietly.

No one answered me.

"Who died!" I demanded.

"Who died!" I screamed.

The words exploded inside my head. The landscape changed, evaporating all around me in a foul vapor. Then I was all alone. The mourners were gone. The carriages were gone. The iron gate was gone and so were the trees and birds, and a terrible silence crushed down around me.

"Who died?" I asked softly. No one was there to hear.

Then a new sound emerged from the depthless silence. Dirt rattled upon wooden boxes. I turned. Two old men were shoveling dirt into the dark holes. I stood beside them a moment, then I saw a third man, standing off to one side, alone. His head was bent toward the holes and his broad shoulders quivered slightly beneath his blue coat, as if under an unbearable strain. He was a young man, tall with gray eyes and a strong, chiseled face. He wore the long, double-breasted frock coat of an army captain, and he was crying. I stepped to his side, knowing a sudden urge to take this sad man into my arms and comfort him. But I didn't.

"Who died?" I asked, gently this time.

I looked into his sad, gray face and something inside me told me I knew this man. I both loved him and hated him at the same time. His hollow cheeks were streaked, but I knew it was proper and fitting that he should be crying now, so I asked him again in a soft voice.

"Who died, sir?"

He raised a long finger and pointed at the three head-stones laying on the ground, carved and waiting to be placed. I went to my knees besides them, touched the cold granite. A lump formed in my throat and I began to sob as I read the names inscribed on each:

Betty Lee Kellogg 1843–1863

Lisa Ann Kellogg 1860–1863

Anna Lee Kellogg 1860–1863

"No!" My brain began to spin, my ears ringing. Somewhere off in the distance a church bell had begun to peal.

Then everything was calm and still. What remained of my rational brain told me that there had been no church bells at the funeral. Why did I hear them now? I wondered.

I could stand it no longer. That bell was summoning me, forcing me back to a place I did not want to go; back from the past.

Back . . . back . . . back . . .

A warm breeze gently stroked my face and the backs of my hands. I inhaled deeply, vaguely aware of the deep ache in my chest; a heaviness that hindered my breathing. I opened my eyes to a cloudy, indistinct world. I couldn't move my head. Something was hold-ing it fast. A wave of panic momentarily surged through me.

When I shut my eyes, a vision swooped over me as

if out of a feverish nightmare. There was that tall girl
in the brown skirt, the gun in her hand, the hollow echo
of its hammer being drawn back. Out the corner of my
mind's eye McGee was lunging at me, but he was moving so slow, so very slow. I heard those words again,
"This is for Joey," then the boom of the gun, and finally
McGee slamming into my shoulder . . . but something
else had hit me first and knocked me off my feet. Laying there on the boardwalk, I felt no pain, nothing at
all, only half-aware of the sun glaring out of the separating clouds in the sky above me, and the hurrying
footsteps all around. McGee's voice reached me, then
faded away and that was all I remembered.

I opened my eyes again and fought to bring them
into focus. Slowly, indistinct shapes began to gather in
the fog, merging into images, the gray tones around me
slowly taking on color. A church bell was ringing from
beyond an open window. I tried turning my head again
and winced as a shot of pain seared my neck. All I
could move was my eyes. I shifted them to the left.
There was a window there, and a warm breeze that
ruffled light, sheer curtains. Sunlight brightened the
room and fell warm upon the bed where I was laying.
My view followed a clean, white wall. An empty chair
sat next to the window, a small table with a pitcher of
water and a glass stood near the bed. Beyond the bed
a tall wood-and-glass cabinet resided against another
wall. It held shelves and bottles and some shiny devices
that were unfamiliar. Suddenly I knew where I was and
wondered how long I'd been here.

A closed door pierced the wall on the far side of the
room, and that was the limit of my view of this place.

My eyes drifted back to the tall cabinet and fixed upon it without really seeing it. As I struggled to sort the confusion that still clouded my thoughts, I was suddenly aware of my terrible thirst. My tongue was a dried piece of leather and my lips like rattlesnake skin. I glanced at the pitcher of water near the bed and tried for it, but nothing worked. My arms were too heavy to lift, and my legs seemed to be made of lead. To make matters worse, someone had contrived a running iron near my head, and every time I moved, it poked me in the neck. That pitcher of water might as well have been a mile away.

My hands rested one atop the other, upon the sheet that covered me. Examining them, I noted that all ten fingers still worked, and for the moment that was all I *was* sure of.

My thirst burned hotter. I wanted the water in that pitcher. I tried to call out for someone, but the exertion was too much. After a few moments I closed my eyes, hearing the voices of folks on the sidewalk beyond the open window, and that incessant church bell ringing . . .

"Cap? . . . Cap?"

McGee's voice called me out of another haunting nightmare. It had been a dark dream that I wanted to be free of, but one that did not want to let go of me. He continued to call and I desperately tried to answer.

"Cap?"

Grudgingly, my eyes opened. McGee's face was hovering over me and his mouth suddenly widened into a smile. "Praise be the saints above!" he proclaimed.

"Water," I croaked, swallowing hard. My voice was a grating whisper, foreign to my ears.

McGee filled the glass and put it gently to my lips. "Can't raise your head none, Cap. Be careful now. Not so fast you'll choke yourself."

Water trickled off my lips, over my chin, and down my neck. I drank the glass dry and asked for more. Afterward, my mouth felt more or less alive again, rattlesnake skin softening a little.

"How you feeling, Cap?"

Laying there half-alive and staring up at the explosion of red hair, I figured that was a dumb question. Shadows darkened the room now. Light from a lamp somewhere shone off the white walls and McGee's beaming face.

"I figured you for a goner, Cap. Praise be the saints, you made it through!" He thanked the saints a couple more times then said, "Doc Perry sure knew what he was doing when he patched you up. Said if it weren't for the fact that you got the constitution of an ornery mule, you'd be dead as a can of corned beef. Yessiree, he did a fine job of patching you up."

When McGee settled down, I asked, "We still in Calico Lace?" and then realized that was a dumb question too.

"Where else did you expect to be after catching a slug in the chest like you done? Be thankful you are still in Calico Lace, and not in the hereafter. You was walking a narrow line there for a while."

"I'm hungry."

"Ain't surprised. You've et noting since Tuesday."

"Tuesday? What day is it?"

"Sunday."

"Sunday!" I grimaced. I'd been unconscious nearly a week. "What have you been doing with yourself while I've been warming this bed?"

"Doing?" He frowned, "Mostly I've been *warming* that there chair, thinking I had lit upon a porcupine. I've been worried sick, listening to you rant and rave 'bout this and that. It was chilling, what with you all the time asking 'Who died?' and other such things as would drive a banshee to fright. I didn't know what to make of it, but the doc said it was to be expected of a man fighting with de-leery-em.

"Folks here in Calico Lace have been mighty concerned about you, Cap. Some of 'em have been peeking in every day just to see how you was doing. You know, they ain't half-bad people once you get to know them."

"Suppose that's true for most folks," I allowed, getting weary again and feeling sleep nudging at my brain.

"I'm pleased to hear you say that, Mr. Kellogg."

A short, portly man with a crown of white hair circling a balding pate and spectacles perched upon his hawkish nose was standing in the doorway. Light from another room showed him in silhouette until he started across the room. He walked with a limp.

"How does it feel to once again be part of the conscious world?" he inquired, wearing a small smile.

"Feels like I have some catching up to do."

"You will have plenty of time for that."

McGee said, "This here is Doc Perry."

"From what McGee tells me, I owe you my life."

He waved a hand. "You owe me nothing, sir. You had as much to do with it as I, you and the Man upstairs." He bent and pulled up my eyelid and peered closely. "That looks much better. Have much pain in the chest, Mr. Kellogg?"

"It feels heavy when I breathe, like I've got a sack of flour atop me. But not much pain. It's my neck that burns like sin."

"Oh that." He seemed unconcerned. "I had to immobilize your head, same as your arms and legs. You had a forty-four slug lodged about half an inch from your heart. It broke a rib and tore up a lot of connective tissue and blood vessels. My scalpel cut more when I operated to remove the bullet and repair what I could. I had to strap you down to this bed to stop you from moving around and causing any more damage than Miss Nelson's bullet had already done. The neck pain is only strained muscles."

He removed the head straps. "That should help. The pain will go away in a day or so."

I rotated my head, already feeling some relief from that burning ache. "How about untying my arms?"

Perry peered gravely at me, considering, then shook his head. "Not right yet, Mr. Kellogg. You have been having some very violent dreams. I wouldn't want to risk you thrashing around in your sleep and tearing your incision."

I frowned and McGee said, "He's the doc, Cap. He knows what's good for you, and I stand by his decision. I wouldn't want to find you bled to dead during the night because of some evil dream. No sir. If Doc Perry says you stay strapped down, then strapped you'll be." He leaned a little closer and added conciliatorily, "It's for your own good, Cap."

I might have argued with Perry, but with McGee on his side, I knew it was hopeless. I was getting too tired to argue anyway. The bed seemed to be gently swaying and my eyelids took on weight. I wasn't going to press the point—at least not tonight, anyway.

As I drifted off I heard Perry say, "He can use all the sleep he can get." I thought that strange since I'd just slept nearly the week away.

"But he just woke up," McGee protested.

"He's suffered considerable trauma. He's lucky to be alive. Let him sleep."

The glow of lamplight took on a red tinge through my closed eyelids. McGee's and Perry's voices moved to the far end of a long tunnel. Their words grew faint and the sound of their footsteps upon the floor reminded me of steam escaping a locomotive's boiler. I wanted to tell them not to leave. I wanted food, but my body demanded sleep too. Sleep won out.

I came suddenly awake and lay there in the quiet darkness listening. Something had pulled me from sleep. I did not move, did not open my eyes, just slowly became aware of breathing coming from the blackness. I slit my eyes and carefully tested my arms. The straps were still in place. I was helpless, and panic rose within me. I resisted it forcibly and wondered if this was part of another dream.

Then a shadow moved. Boots scraped the floor and a tall figure materialized at the foot of my bed. The glow of moonlight through the window faintly outlined him against the blackness of the room. My heart was pounding, but I pretended to be asleep. I was helpless, but the man only stood there, watching me from the shadows, his shallow breathing sounding like a whirl-wind to my brain. Time passed. I don't know how much. I was drifting off again and I fought against it.

The man suddenly backed away. Perhaps he had seen me stir. He turned abruptly and hurried out the dark doorway. As he left, I caught a glimpse of his hat in the moonlight—wide and flat-brimmed, with a high Montana crown . . .

Then he was gone.

7

IT WAS ONLY another dream, I told myself, afraid to open my eyes, afraid the nightmare might still be lurking there at the foot of my bed. I wondered briefly what had come to haunt me this time, but as sleep left me I became aware that something was different. It was no mysterious breathing in the dark summoning me back to consciousness, but the song of a meadowlark riding upon warm, pine-scented air, and it filled me with a peace I'd not known for a long time.

I kept my eyes shut, fearing the sensation would leave me once I opened them. Now there was something else. My mind began to conjure up visions of bacon, fried eggs, and coffee—rich black coffee!

I could stand it no longer. I had to find out. I had to take that chance . . .

"Good morning, Mr. Kellogg," Her voice was soft and friendly. It came from the chair beside the bed. I turned toward it, the pain in my neck now just a dull reminder of what it had been.

Mary Kenyon smiled at me. Her long brown hair was pulled back and held in place with a yellow ribbon that matched the color of her dress. She had been wearing white gloves that she now clutched in one small hand upon her lap. The other hand was pressed gently to her neck, long fingers seemingly guarding her throat as she leaned forward, concern filling her wide eyes.

"How are you feeling, Mr. Kellogg?" she asked softly.

I recalled that McGee had asked me that same question. It had irritated me at the time, but somehow Mary asking it did not affect me at all that way. I rubbed my cardboard lips with my boot-leather tongue and said, "There is a pitcher of water and a glass on the table behind you, ma'am."

She filled the glass and lifted my head, propping a pillow behind it. "Not too fast," she said, helping me.

I gulped it just the same, managing between swallows to tell her how dry I had been lately.

"The doctor says you lost a lot of fluids and it will take time to replace them."

"If feeling like I've just crawled out of a desert means I've lost fluids, then I reckon the doc knows what he is talking about." We sat there a moment looking at each other as an uncomfortable silence came over us. To break it I said, "When I woke just now I thought I smelled bacon and eggs. I'm hoping I wasn't just having another dream."

Her face beamed and she said, "Eggs, bacon, coffee, and biscuits." The glow dimmed a bit. "But I'm afraid the doctor disapproves. I really should have asked him before I brought it over. I promised I'd call him just as soon as you woke up." She smiled again. "I'll be right back."

As she disappeared through the doorway, I was struck again by her beauty. Mary Kenyon cut a fine figure of a woman. She came back with Dr. Perry almost at once. He looked me over and said my color was much improved. I wasn't concerned about my color, only my empty stomach.

"I think we can remove these now," Perry said, unbuckling the leather belts across my arms and legs. He and Mary carefully raised me into a sitting position, stuffing pillows against the wall to keep me that way.

"I must've had a better night," I said, watching his face.

"Better?"

"You said you'd remove these if I did."

"Oh, yes, quite right. I didn't hear a peep out of you all night."

"You spent the whole night keeping an eye on me?"

"No, no. I turned in around midnight. You didn't experience any discomfort, did you?" he asked, concerned.

I told him I didn't, wondering if my night visitor wasn't just one more bad dream. I glanced around the room, pausing on the doorway. "You live here, I presume."

"Yes, indeed. My rooms are right above you." He stabbed a finger at the ceiling then, smiling, changed the subject. "Miss Kenyon has brought you a hearty breakfast, but I'm not so sure your system is ready for so much solid food. I'd much prefer you start with a bowl of broth." He grinned. "But if I don't let her mother you like she wants, I fear you might have to move over and make room for me in that sickbed."

"Doctor!" she said, her cheeks flushing.

Perry laughed quietly and nodded his head two or three times. "I will be in my office should you need anything. Actually, some bacon and eggs shouldn't hurt so long as you go easy on them the next few days." He shifted his view to Mary. "I'll depend on you to take charge here. Feed him lightly and only one cup of coffee." Giving her a wink, Perry limped out the door.

"That man," she scoffed, but with affection.

"The doctor seems a thoughtful gentleman. Very concerned."

"Dr. Perry is a darling, but he's an old busybody." Her nose wrinkled with a smile.

"I'd call it perceptive."

She looked at me curiously, then reached for a basket on the floor beside the bed. "Mr. McGee tells me you are a man about to starve to death."

"McGee is perceptive too. By the way, where is he?"

Her shoulders rolled beneath the yellow dress as she began unpacking the basket. "I don't know. When I was coming here I saw him and Matt Stringer riding out of town. Cliff Nelson was with them," she added, looking up. I had the feeling that last part was supposed to mean something to me. It didn't.

Mary tucked a napkin into the gown I was wearing and went on quickly, "But I suspect he will be back shortly. Mr. McGee has been very faithful, sitting here and waiting, just waiting and watching. He hardly ate anything at all. I brought him food from the café whenever I came by. I suppose, now that you are on the mend, Mr. McGee will be about other business."

"I suppose," I agreed, "if we had any other business here in Calico Lace. We were only passing through, on our way to Fountain Colony."

"Yes, I heard. You are a railroad surveyor." She uncovered a steaming plate, and the delicious odor almost overwhelmed me. I didn't know how hungry I really was, and suddenly all I could think about was eating. Mary helped me, serving portions according to Perry's instructions.

"McGee wasn't exaggerating when he said you were starving." She poured coffee from a small carafe and put it in my hands. It was no longer hot, but I wolfed it down anyway.

"First food I've had since this happened." I was feeling better already. "Not surprising I'm not better yet. But a few helpings of your good cooking should get me on my feet directly."

She laughed. "It will take more than three squares a day to get you fit again. But we've made a good start."

"Yes, ma'am." I wiped my lips and held out the coffee cup.

Mary took it from me, shaking her head. "Only one. You heard the doctor."

"I'll never tell."

When she smiled, her brown eyes had a sparkle to them that nearly took my breath. I tried not to stare. "No. Maybe he won't know, but I will."

"Good looks, and integrity too."

Her sudden scowl told me she didn't like that. But she covered it over quickly and said, "I want you to get better, not worse, Mr. Kellogg."

"Jacob," I heard myself say. "Mr. Kellogg was my father." Our relationship was changing. She felt it too. Her eyes told me so. She turned quickly away and began repacking the wicker basket.

When she finished, she said, "I have to leave. I do have a business to run." Her voice was suddenly gentle. "The most important thing now is for you to get a lot of rest and get better."

"I've been resting all week. Have you no pity? Stay, just a little longer."

"You are still a very sick man, Mist—Jacob." She paused, then smiled. "I will drop back this evening and see how you are doing. Is there anything I can get you before I leave?"

I glanced at the pitcher of water. "Can you fill that glass for me, and move the table where I can reach it?"

Mary did, then she touched my hand. "You get better, now," she said, and left me with a bright farewell smile that held all kinds of promise. I stared at the doorway long after she had gone, considering. After deliberating on it, I decided there was really no good reason for her to befriend me. I was a stranger here, and, beyond a coincidental resemblance to a character of ill repute, Mary didn't know me from Adam. For that matter, I didn't know her from Eve. It was an equally limited basis to begin a friendship, but it was a beginning. There was no denying the attraction I felt, and I was certain she had felt it too.

McGee and I were just passing through, I reminded myself. I didn't even like this town . . . Calico Lace . . . what kind of a name was that anyway? As if to buttress that notion, a vision of a tall, slender woman loomed into view.

This is for Joey.

Joey?

Hadn't Sheriff Griever mentioned that name? I tried to recall, but my memories were all jumbled up, confused by the events that had followed. Just then Dr. Perry stuck his head in the doorway and I temporarily shelved the problem.

"Just checking," he said, swinging his stiff leg and stopping by my bed. "Breakfast sit well?"

"I'm not feeling so much like an empty drum," I said.

"You needed that."

"What I need is to get back on my feet. How long am I going to be stuck in this bed?"

Perry snorted. "Impatient man, aren't you? You're lucky to be *stuck* in that bed at all. It beats a hole in the ground."

I grinned. "No argument there. It's just I'm not used to spending time flat on my back."

"I suggest you get used to it, Mr. Kellogg." Perry lowered his stocky frame onto the edge of the bed and turned back the sheet. It was my first glimpse at the bandages that encircled my chest. A wide, crusted stain of dried blood colored the wrappings. I grimaced, trying not to think about what I looked like beneath them.

"To tell you the truth, I really didn't expect you to pull through. I've seen plenty of men hurt less than yourself not make it." Perry rose and went to the cabinet. He removed a porcelain bowl and a pair of scissors and put them on the little table. He left the room, but was back in a few minutes carrying a kettle of hot water. He filled the bowl.

"Let's see what it looks like," he said, snipping at the wrappings. "You know, a few years back you would have never survived an ordeal such as this. It wasn't so long ago that when we cut open a man, like I had to open you up, he usually died. Not so much from the operation, but from the infection that would set in. Then a few years ago a surgeon in London, England, by the name of Joseph Lister discovered that by using Phenol, a weak carbolic acid, to disinfect the skin before surgery, we could prevent much of the infection. Phenol now allows doctors to do surgery that would formerly have been fatal. You do not know how lucky you are, Mr. Kellogg. Don't complain over having to spend a few weeks in bed."

Perry peeled back the top layer of bandages and placed a wet cloth over the gauze stuck to the wound. "This will soften it some," he said.

"Just what am I supposed to do for the next few weeks?"

Perry lowered his head and peered at me over the rim of his eyesglasses. "You play chess?"

"Never have."

"Want to learn?"

"I'm game. You play poker?"

He chuckled. "It's going to cost you plenty when you get my bill, Mr. Kellogg. It wouldn't be ethical for me to steal your money too. Does horrendous things to the blood pressure." He lifted away the damp cloth and snipped the few remaining threads that still clung to the scabby flesh. "There, that should do it."

A blazing red scar, like a fat night crawler, crawled across my chest. The skin was puffy and swollen, held together with stitches every quarter of an inch; the knotted ends of the threads sticking up like a row of coarse whiskers. Perry examined it, nodding approvingly.

"Beautiful," he murmured softly. "See," he went on, pointing a finger, "not a sign of pus anywhere, just good, healthy tissue. Beautiful!"

"Beautiful, Doc," I mumbled, and had to look away.

"Phenol!" he declared. "Thank God for men like Lister. Mark my words, Mr. Kellogg, history will not soon forget him." He lightly draped a piece of gauze over the wound. "I'm going to leave it open to the air for the time being. It will help it to heal." Perry unbuckled the remaining straps around my legs. "Won't be needing these any longer."

I was grateful to be able to move my legs. I stretched and he said, "Tomorrow we will get you up on your feet for a few minutes. The sooner you start using your muscles, the better you will feel." He bent for something under the bed and came up with a curiously shaped metal pan. "Now that you are conscious and can move around a bit under your own power, you can be of great help to me." He explained how to maneuver the pan into position and then get it out again without spilling it. "When you are finished just set it on the floor and I'll take it from there."

I frowned. "How about I just use the privy out back?"

"Maybe in a few days." Perry gathered up the old bandages, put them in the porcelain bowl, and tossed the scissors in after them. "I'll be back a little later to check in on you, Mr. Kellogg," he said, and left.

I laid there awhile staring at the ceiling and thinking. The warm morning breeze that ruffled the curtains was sweet with the scent of pine trees. I *was* grateful to be alive, and wondered why it had to take nearly being killed to realize it. My thoughts skipped around, but eventually settled down on Mary Kenyon.

She was a puzzlement. Why was she so concerned over my well-being? As I considered this, my brain switched tracks to that tall girl in the brown riding skirt. Who was she? And who was Joey? It suddenly occurred to me that neither Mary nor Perry had mentioned her. Surely they knew who the trigger-happy woman was. Surely she was sitting in the local jail right now. I was suddenly irritated. I was a prisoner in this bed, and no one was telling me what I was entitled to know. I made a note to start asking more questions for that was the only way, it seemed, that I was going to get the answers.

8

VOICES FROM BEYOND the open doorway brought me awake. I recognized McGee's gruff laugh instantly, but it took me a few moments to match Sheriff Griever's face to the other. I'd been asleep, I realized, and wondered how long. Long shadows filled the room. The window was closed and someone had pulled a light blanket up to my neck.

From outside the doorway Perry's soft voice said, "He has been asleep all afternoon, and he needs it. I don't want to disturb him if it isn't absolutely necessary."

"I understand, Doc," Griever replied easily. "When would be a good time?"

"Try tomorrow, around nine, after he has had some breakfast. He's recovering nicely." Perry gave a short laugh. "He is going to live, Thad. That should lift a big burden off of your shoulders."

"Well, Doc, I know of one man who is going to be mighty pleased to hear that."

McGee's voice broke in. "Make that two men, Sheriff."

"Make that three," I murmured quietly, listening to them talking just beyond the doorway. I could have seen the sheriff just then, but something inside me refused to call out. I was stuck in this bed for the duration, so to speak, and I might as well spread the visitors out. A few weeks, Perry had said. If I used them up all up front, I could find myself all by my lonesome the last week of my confinement. The idea of playing chess with Doc Perry, or staring into McGee's face for a whole week with no other diversion did little to thrill me.

Griever told Perry good-bye. I heard the scuff of his boots and the creak of a door opening then closing someplace beyond my little, one-room world. McGee said he would just take a chair and wait for me to wake up. I closed my eyes and heard him shuffle in and settle himself by the side of my bed.

"Did you and Stringer have a nice ride?"

"You're awake."

"I heard the three of you out there. It's a comfort to know so many people have taken an interest in my recovery." The odor of whiskey reached me. I opened my eyes and looked at McGee's flushed face. "You've been drinking."

"Celebrating, Cap."

I gave him a narrowed look. "Celebrating? While your old captain is flat on his back teetering between life and death?"

"Life and death?" he scoffed. "Don't give me that. Doc Perry says you are gonna heal up good as new.

No, I was celebrating because you were on the mend."

"I'm touched, truly touched, McGee."

He frowned. "I ain't gonna hear no more of this, Cap. I was having me a drink with Mr. Nelson. Mr. Cliff Nelson."

"Nelson?" He had said the name like it was supposed to mean something to me. So had Mary this morning, I recalled.

"He owns the C-N Ranch, what borders the Iron Ridge—Matt Stringer's land." McGee leaned back in the chair, a smile crawling across his face. "Don't that beat all?"

"Wait a minute. I've been trying to put some name together all day. Nelson? Joey? Joey Nelson? The boy the sheriff told us about. The one John Carver badgered into a gunfight." I stopped to think it through. "The girl who shot me. She said, 'This is for Joey.' "

McGee nodded. "You've got it figured out, Cap. Joey is—err, was, Cliff Nelson's son."

But I didn't have it figured out. "Okay, so who is the girl?"

McGee's eyes widened in surprise. "Mean you don't know?"

"Know? Nobody has told me anything yet!"

"The gal who shot you, why, that was Joey's sister, Penny Nelson, Cliff's daughter. 'Cept her pa don't call her Penny. No-sir-ee, calls her Penelda Ann. A mighty fancy handle for such a hellcat, I say.

"Her old man, Cliff, will be mighty happy to hear you are going to live. He's been in a sweat, not knowing which way the boot was gonna drop. They've just been waiting so they can charge Penny accordingly. If you had gone under, it would be murder; now it looks like attempted murder will be the charge."

McGee frowned. "But the way I see it, Cap, that gal likely would never have seen a jury. The sheriff didn't even throw her behind bars. He just toted her home to her papa for what I reckon must have been a good spanking. Considering the circumstances, what with you looking like this Carver fellow, and sentiments being what they are toward him, I got the feeling folks were prepared to handle this like it was just some unfortunate accident."

"Unfortunate," I mused. "Where is this Miss Penelda Ann Nelson now?"

"Out to the ranch house, under lock and key, I suspect. Her pa is keeping an eagle eye on her."

"Is that where you and Matt Stringer rode off to earlier today?"

"We did. Remember Matt saying he had some land needing to be surveyed? Well, I figured since you and me was stuck here for who knows how long, I might as well get busy and make some money. I took the job. We was out looking over the countryside. Pretty rugged, but we've shot lines through worse.

"Afterward, we rode over to the Nelson place. He calls it a ranch, but it ain't really. Four or five years ago when the gold mines started opening up, Nelson sold off nearly all his cows and built himself a crusher mill to process the ore from the surrounding mines. Reckon he figured there was more money to be made in gold than in beef. He calls it the Verna Mae Mill, after his wife, you see. The mill operates 'round the clock, and according to Stringer, Cliff used to send off a wagon load of gold amalgam to Castle Rock twice a month, to ship it out on the railroad. But he says Cliff's been having troubles of some kind. Gold hasn't gone out for a while.

"He still runs a few cows too, for old times' sake, he says, but he doesn't even ship them to market. Doubt they butcher but two or three a year for their own pots. They treat them animals more like the family dog than livestock. He even gives 'em names, by gosh!"

Perry poked his head into the room. "I thought I heard the two of you confabulating," he said good-naturedly. "You've got a visitor, Mr. Kellogg, and a mighty pretty one at that."

"Oh, Doc!" Mary's voice scolded in the background. She came into the room carrying that wicker basket of food. "I brought you something to eat. Are you feeling up to it?"

"Does a coyote feel up to howling?" McGee snickered.

"I seem to have slept right through lunch."

"I know," she said gently.

McGee leaped up and offered her his chair.

"Thank you, Mr. McGee," she replied, lowering herself gracefully into it. "I've brought you roast beef and a baked potato, and some cherry cobbler. It's today's specialty."

She was wearing the same yellow dress, and the same yellow ribbon was keeping her long, brown hair away from her face. But her crisp, fresh appearance of this morning was missing, replaced by an air of wilted, disheveled exhaustion. Her face was tired, and weariness dulled her eyes, but the smile was still bright and cheerful. That never-changing smile. I wondered how she managed it. At the moment, tired as she looked, it seemed a little unreal, a little unnatural.

"I hope I didn't interrupt anything important," she said, shifting her view between McGee and myself. The long stare that lingered upon McGee suggested that three was going to be a crowd. "I heard you two talking and didn't want to barge in, but I didn't want to bring you a cold dinner either."

"You didn't interrupt anything," I said. "McGee was just telling me all about the girl responsible for my extended visit here in your friendly town. The only one so far to take the time to explain it to me."

Mary's eyelids fluttered and turned down to the basket on her lap. Then she opened it and quickly removed a napkin, silverware, and a warm plate, arranging them on the table. "I wasn't aware you hadn't been told," she said, "and I didn't think it my place to mention it."

I was sorry I had mentioned it. "You're right. I guess I'm just a little edgy."

Her smile told me I was forgiven. The wonderful odor of the food drew my eyes. "That smells like Heaven, ma'am. How am I ever going to repay you for your kindness?"

"You don't have to repay me, Mr. Kellogg—"

"Jacob," I corrected.

She smiled. "I'd be remiss in my Christian duty if I did not care for the sick."

"Is that why you are being so kind to me?"

Mary flushed. Our eyes met briefly before she looked away. "Of course not."

McGee chuckled. "Just make out a bill for all this food and make it a big one."

I gave him a curious look. "Mighty generous, aren't you? Doc Perry's bill alone is liable to keep us here in bondage for years, paying it off."

"Now that is an interesting idea," Mary allowed.

I looked at McGee, who was trying to hold back a smirk. "You are about to choke on whatever it is you are gloating on. What is it?"

"I was just about to tell you that, Cap. Mr. Nelson says he's going to pick up the bill for this whole she-bang. Says it's the least he can do, considering it was his kid that put you here."

"Why, that's wonderful," Mary declared. "It is only right that he should."

I wasn't so sure. "I don't know, I don't like owing anyone."

She looked incredulous. "If anybody owes anyone, it is he owing you, Mr. Kellogg."

"She's right," McGee put in.

I studied her tired face and said, "I thought we settled that this morning." That took her by surprise. She looked suddenly worried and I had to laugh in spite of the pain it caused me. "Jacob. Mr. Kellogg was my father."

Then she smiled. "I forgot."

Doc Perry stuck his head into the room. "I just heard what Mr. McGee said. I was going to go easy on you. Maybe I'll take you up on that poker game after all." He chuckled and disappeared again.

Mary said, "With that good news, I'm sure you won't have any trouble eating your dinner."

"What makes you think I'd have trouble eating your cooking? Anyway, I'm so hungry right now I could eat in the middle of Pickett's Gettysburg Charge!"

She frowned. "Don't go bringing up that past, Jacob. It isn't good for you."

I made a wry smile. "The present hasn't been all that healthy either," I reminded her.

9

PERRY HITCHED AN arm around my waist and grunted softly as he took my weight upon his shoulder. "If it begins to hurt much, we can postpone this," he said, straightening up. "There is no profit in rushing this."

"I'm all right," I said, leaning onto his shoulder and letting him ease me off the edge of the bed. My legs were shaky. I concentrated on keeping them firmly beneath me and battled against stiff joints to rise to my full six-foot-three inches.

"What are you feeling in your incision?"

"Hurts a little, like the skin won't stretch."

"That's to be expected." I took my first step. "It will require some pulling and stretching of that scar to get the skin back to the right size. Just think of it like putting a dart in a shirt."

I grinned. "Only problem is, Doc, that shirt fitted just fine before you went to sewing on it."

"This is why I wanted you up on your feet as soon

as possible." Perry helped me hobble around the room. It was slow going, but then I wasn't in any hurry. Just being out of bed and standing on my own two pins was an accomplishment. As we passed the foot of the bed, I looked at the rumpled sheets and remembered the dream—that dark figure who had stood in this very place, hidden by night shadows . . . watching, just watching. Did it really happen? Or *was* it just another of those nightmares? At the time it had seemed frighteningly real, but now it was only a question that lingered at the back of my brain. I glanced away, at the open doorway where my "dream" had hurried out.

"Where does that lead, Doc?" I asked, inclining my head.

"That is my office."

"And beyond?"

"The rest of the house—a parlor, the kitchen, my library. There is a staircase to the second floor, where my rooms are. In a few days I'll take you on the grand tour. You should be up to it by then. You're making great strides." We came back around to the bed again and he said, "Well, that should be enough for today."

I recoiled at the thought of getting back in bed and asked if I could sit in the chair, by the window, for a few minutes. Perry considered my request, and it must not have been too unreasonable because he finally nodded and said, "I don't suppose that would hurt you."

He helped me into the chair and I had my first glimpse of Calico Lace through the window of my room . . . My world was expanding. Outside Dr. Perry's house, a low picket fence surrounded a small front yard, braced on either side by two tall fir trees. Beyond them lay the main street of Calico Lace running a direction I didn't recognize at first. It took me a moment to orient myself from this new angle. I studied the row of buildings marching along the road, the very last one visible from my vantage point being the Kenyon Café. Noting it, I got a bearing on the rest of the town. The hotel had to be several storefronts away on my left—on this side of the street. Hiram's Livery was two or three buildings to my right; Millford's Saloon was not visible from this point, but I knew it was not more than thirty or forty feet west of Mary's café.

The morning was bright and warm, and the sound of birds mingled with the jangle of harnesses and traces, the rumble of wagon wheels, and the occasional voice that made it this far.

"Can I interest you in a game of chess?" Perry asked.

"No, thanks, not right now," I said with my eyes still turned out the window. "I just want to sit here awhile and watch, and enjoy the morning." I grinned. "Surprising how big the little pleasures become when you are laid up for a while."

"I'll be off, then. Give me a holler if you need anything."

I heard Perry's hobbled gait shuffle out of the room. I watched two squirrels chase each other around the trunk of one of the firs until they scampered away. The odor of bakery bread mingled with the distant smell of manure. Somewhere a windmill was clacking, gushing water into a barrel. Riders and the occasional freight wagon would appear then vanish around a corner.

I was watching two women chatting their way along

the boardwalk when I spied Mary Kenyon step from her eatery, the familiar wicker basket over her arm. She had started up the street when suddenly a man stepped out from a side alley and beckoned to her. They obviously knew each other, but I couldn't help noticing the sudden grave look that cast itself over Mary's face when she saw him. She glanced quickly up and down the street then slipped into the alley with him. I could only barely make them out in the shadows. They spoke a few minutes then I saw the man nod his head and disappear deeper into the alley.

As Mary resumed her journey toward Doc Perry's house, her smile now seemed faded, her jaw unusually tight, showing a determination that seemed somehow out of place on her pretty face.

As I watched her cross the street with her basket over her arm, I looked down at the bandages wrapped about my half-naked body and it suddenly occurred to me that I was not properly attired to receive lady visitors. I called Perry, who helped me back into bed and under the sheets. As he fixed the pillow behind my head I was aware of a certain anticipation, and it irked me that I could not truthfully say whether it was due to the imminent arrival of Mary, or the food I knew she was bringing.

"Jacob . . ." Her voice was like honey, her laugh a melody to ease a tired soul. She was collecting the dirty dishes, repacking them in the basket. "I am so pleased with your progress. Walking around, even? That is wonderful." She paused and straightened the white bonnet on her head. "It is hard to believe that only a

week ago . . ." Her words trailed off, a frown momentarily smothering the smile. "I'm sorry, darling, I didn't
mean to bring that up."

Somewhere between the time Mary had arrived and
now, our relationship had taken another subtle turn. It
was no longer Mr. Kellogg, or even Jacob. Now she
had slipped into the almost too comfortable use of *darling*. Betty had never called me that, even after five
years of marriage. She had been a practical woman
whose concerns in life had been her children, her husband, and the farm—in that order. Anything frivolous
had not been part of Betty's world. She owned one
good hat and one good dress appropriate for church,
weddings, and funerals. Three other dresses made due
for farm chores. She had been a hardworking woman
who firmly believed that if your name was Jacob, or
Pete or Harry, then that was what the Good Lord intended you to be called. Other than the twins, Betty
never called anyone *darling*.

I watched Mary preparing to leave and knew it had
not been the food in her basket that had stirred that
certain sense of anticipation within me earlier. Mary
was both beguiling and appealing. Life had suddenly
become complicated and I was getting that old, familiar
itch to saddle up and leave—just like past times. But
now there was a catch. I couldn't even get out of bed
without help, let alone saddle my horse and hightail it
out of town. Fate seemed to be forcing me to see this
through.

"I must be off, darling," she said, adjusting the tilt
of her hat, "but I'll see you later. In the meantime, you
just work at getting better." She bent and patted my

hand with gloved fingers. A peck on the cheek would have been appropriate, but the relationship hadn't progressed that far yet, and for that I was thankful. As it was, things were moving faster than I liked.

Mary left with a rustling of skirts across the floor, briefly turning from the door to throw a farewell smile over her shoulder at me. She left and I discovered I was grinning. Maybe I had just been too long without a woman. I could think of no other reason why she should have captivated me so quickly and thoroughly. Mary was nothing at all like Betty had been.

I heard Mary speak to Doc Perry, her words muffled as if spoken from beyond Perry's office. Perry's chuckle came through loud and clear, though, and then another voice.

"I'm pleased you are taking such good care of him, ma'am. Is he up to seeing another visitor?" I recognized the voice as belonging to the sheriff.

Her reply to too soft for me to hear. He said, "Now, don't fret. I won't keep him long." Then Thad Griever was on his way in.

His tall, thin frame came through the doorway. A wide smile brightened his face and long, nut brown fingers clasped the brim of his hat in his fists. "Mary was right. You're looking good as a crisp fifty-dollar bill, Mr. Kellogg." Griever tossed the hat upon the table, turned the chair around, and straddled it with his long legs, crossing his arms over its back.

I gave him a rueful grin and said, "Cliff Nelson will be relieved when you tell him."

Griever's smile faltered a bit. "We are all relieved, Mr. Kellogg. Calico Lace is a respectable town, and when something like this happens, well, it reflects badly on all of us. You know what they say about one bad apple." He paused and his blue eyes filled with concern. "You have a way of reaching right in at a sore spot and giving a tug."

"A sore spot? You mean the Nelsons? Penny Nelson in particular? Or should I call her Penelda Ann, like her old man does?"

Griever grimaced. "Sure you ain't a reader for one of them traveling carnival shows, Mr. Kellogg? You just gave that tender place a real hard pull. But the Nelson's aren't the reason why I stopped by—well, not the only reason. I was concerned too."

"I appreciate that, Sheriff. According to McGee, a lot of folks are concerned. I'm sorry if I'm being short with you."

"Well, can't hardly blame you for being mad. Like I said, what happened to you was an awful injustice, and a poor reflection on all of us. A lot of folks are embarrassed something like this could happen here, and they are . . . well, just a mite perplexed."

"Perplexed?" I asked. "Perplexed because the trigger-happy girl happens to be the daughter of one of your neighbors?"

"There you go again, pulling at the sore spot. It's not as though she is that bad apple I mentioned earlier. That was aimed at your look-alike. Penny is basically a fine woman, just kinda high-spirited. I can't completely blame her for trying to avenge her brother's death, though what she did was against the law. If it were me, and I wasn't the law in these parts, I might take to a little avenging of the death of a brother myself."

"A little avenging?" My anger began boiling up and I struggled to keep it down. "I'd hate to see what you considered big avenging, Sheriff."

He grimaced. "Sorry. Bad choice of words. Don't go getting all red in the face, Mr. Kellogg. Don't want to see you take a turn now that you're on a healing course."

"That would really upset things around here, wouldn't it?" I shot back. "You might find some way to overlook attempted murder, but a cold body in hand would make matters really difficult." I was feeling particularly vexed with Griever this morning and I didn't know why.

The sheriff frowned and shrugged his thin shoulders. "Like I said, it's a problem. I don't really want to toss that gal in jail." He paused and let me think about it.

I brooded over this awhile, even though I knew he was probably right. If the tables had been turned, would I have let my brother's murderer roam free without taking matters into my own hands? Probably not. It is just that when you are the one flat on your back recovering from a bullet meant for someone who happened to look like you, it is kind of hard not to be narrow-minded on the matter.

"Don't worry about it, Sheriff," I said finally, "I won't press charges. All I want to do is get back on my feet and on my way again."

That must have been what the old man was waiting to hear. His long face brightened and a small grin lifted the corners of his mouth. "I was hoping you'd say that,

Mr. Kellogg. Just the same, I want you to know that if you had decided to press charges, I'd have backed you up on them, in spite of my personal feeling on the matter."

"Thanks," I said coolly.

He cleared his throat. "I can understand your hostility. All I ask is you give us a chance to make it up to you."

It was a reasonable request and Griever seemed a reasonable man. I didn't know why I should be taking out my pent-up anger on him. Maybe it was because there wasn't anyone else at the moment. Being peppery with Mary was unthinkable considering all the care she had shown me, and the same with Doc Perry. That left only Griever. And that was unfortunate because Griever was a sincere, likable man. "All right," I said. "Part of it is being laid up like I am. It's enough to fry anyone's nerves."

"I can understand that too. Once spent two weeks in bed from a half dozen buckshot pellets in my bacon. After a couple days Millie grew right skittish even to bring me my dinner. I'd chew her out 'cause the potatoes were too hard, or the meat too red, or any little thing. I became a real bear to be around, all because I felt plain useless laying there on my back. I know what you are saying, Mr. Kellogg. I understand more than you think."

The way he said it, I almost felt guilty for getting myself shot. There was a benevolence about him that somehow made me more introspective than usual—or maybe it was just that I had a lot more time on my hands to be introspective with.

"The doc tells me you were up on your feet already." Griever fished a plug of tobacco from his vest pocket and shoved it inside his cheek.

"If you can call it that. He walked me around the room a couple times, but he did all the lifting and most of the moving. I just sort of hung on and tried not to fall."

"It's something. It's an improvement. One step at a time, that's how you will be doing it from now until you stroll out of here under your own head of steam."

"Anything would be an improvement," I noted. "Just opening my eyes this morning was an improvement, Sheriff."

He laughed. "Reckon that's a fact," he said. "You've come a long way, but then you could not have started from a much deeper hole, could you? I spoke to Perry before stepping in here. Didn't want to barge in on you, you know. Doc's mighty proud as to the way you're coming round. We all are." Griever lapsed into silence, and suddenly there wasn't anything left to say.

He stood and snatched his hat off the table. "Well, I best be off. I've got work to do." He started for the doorway, then stopped and turned back. "I almost forgot. Cliff Nelson was by my office last night. He wants to cover all your expenses for this . . . this unfortunate mistake."

"McGee mentioned that already."

"Did Mr. McGee also mention that Cliff has invited you out to his ranch to recuperate once you are well enough to travel?"

"No, reckon he forgot to mention that."

"It will be some time before you can ride again, even

after you're up on your feet. Cliff figures you'll be more comfortable out at the ranch. It's a big house, lots of room, and Verna is a real personable woman. It might be good for you. Think it over."

Griever left and I spent some time staring at the ceiling, thinking. Maybe I had been too quick to judge the folks of Calico Lace. They seemed to be trying extra hard to patch up bad feelings. And now I had an invitation from the father of my assailant to recuperate in his home. It all gave me more questions than answers.

I don't know how long I laid there staring. I must have dozed off, for the next thing I was aware of was Mary's gentle touch upon my shoulder.

"Jacob? Are you awake?" came her soft voice.

"What?"

"I didn't mean to startle you. I brought lunch." She began unpacking the basket, but I was only vaguely interested in the food. My mind had been busy ever since Griever left, and I wished McGee was here to answers some of the questions it had come up with.

10

THE NEXT SEVERAL days passed at a snail's pace as I settled down into a routine that would bore the ears off a blind army mule. In the morning I'd take a walk around my room . . . around Perry's office . . . visit the kitchen, the parlor, the office, my room again, my bed. Then I'd count the ceiling tiles until Mary showed up with breakfast over her arm and a smile. There was always that. She arrived precisely the same time every day—breakfast, lunch, dinner. I'd chat with her . . . sit by the window and stare outside . . . eat lunch . . . chat . . . sit and stare some more . . . eat dinner . . . chat . . . lose a game of chess, win a game of poker . . . go to bed . . . sleep fitfully . . . and start all over again.

McGee was still out surveying for Matt Stringer, and as the days passed I felt more and more isolated, growing depressed. The walls began to crush in on me. Cabin fever, it is called, and I was beginning to suspect it was more deadly than the bullet that had tagged me two weeks earlier.

Two weeks, I mused, sitting by the window. Could it really have been that long? I was getting in and out of bed under my own power by this time, and even climbing into my britches by myself. Doc had let me struggle up the staircase this morning on my own to visit the bedrooms on the second floor. I was getting desperate for a change of scenery. Any change! The window was my only link with the outside world, and time spent in the chair looking out it had become precious. For hours I would watch folks coming and going, desperately wanting to be one of them.

It was nearly time for lunch, and I didn't need a clock to tell me that. I had the routine down. I knew instinctively when Mary would step out the front door of her café, her arm hooked through that basket, a pleasant smile upon her face. Even as I thought it, she appeared. "Right on schedule," I murmured to myself as she began her three-times-a-day trek to Doc Perry's house. I watched her without really seeing her. It's not that I was getting weary of her visits. They were a bright spot in an otherwise gloomy existence. It was just that I was getting tired of the whole, dragged out affair. I was tired of everything!

Mary started across the street, then stopped abruptly and turned her head toward the alleyway. She reversed her steps. I shifted my view, but the shadows pretty much hid the man there from me. Mary paused at the mouth of the alley and waited for him to step into the sunlight. He was young, maybe early twenties, I guessed. He shaded his eyes with his hand as the two of them talked. I strained to hear, but they were too far off for that. But they weren't so far that I couldn't get a good look at his face, mainly what was visible beneath the hand perched above his eyes, and the dusty gray hat above that. He wore a full mustache that dropped down past his mouth to his chin. It was a fine-looking mustache for a fellow of his young years, but its splendor paled compared to the bright, shiny conchos that encircled his polished, black leather gun holster. Sunlight reflected off them, dazzling and making the fellow appear bigger than life. But the truth of the matter was, even with the high, undershot riding heals of his boots, he stood no taller than Mary. Though Mary was tall for a woman, a man her height would only be considered of medium size, or even a whisker on the short side.

It occurred to me just then that this was the same fellow who had stopped Mary a week before. I saw him more clearly this time. A week had done much to sharpen my awareness. Thinking it over, I realized it *had* been exactly a week. And exactly a week previous to the first time, Penny Nelson's bullet had laid me flat. Tuesday, Tuesday, and now, Tuesday again. Was it all just a coincidence?

I was making much of nothing, I decided. Coincidence can account for a lot of things so long as you don't try and stretch it too far. Maybe he was a bashful boyfriend, or even a shy brother. Maybe he met her like this all the time, and I had just never noticed it before.

Being cooped up makes a man clutch at straws for

diversion—any kind of diversion. I wondered if it wouldn't be good for me to spend a couple weeks with the Nelsons. The change would probably do me good.

Mary turned away as the man slipped back into the alleyway and disappeared into the shadows. It was nothing, I told myself, watching her resume her trek to Doc Perry's house. Nothing . . . but I couldn't help but notice the determined set of Mary's jaw now as she drew near, and that same hard line of her lips that I had seen before; so out of tune with her otherwise amiable personality. There was a cloud of trouble that dulled the sparkle in her eyes . . . just like the first time.

Two days later Doc Perry gave me the news I'd been waiting to hear. I was fit enough to travel, and if I wanted to, in the morning I could take Cliff Nelson up on his offer. I said I was ready, and that a change of scenery was exactly what I needed. He said he'd pass the word. Later, McGee came back with forty dollars in his pocket and a whole week's worth of news. When I told him I was going to finish my convalescence with the Nelsons, he was delighted. We talked most of the afternoon, and when Mary showed up with dinner, McGee excused himself saying he was going to get a bite to eat.

"Stop by the café and tell Julie I said dinner was on the house," Mary told him.

"Thank you, ma'am," he said and beamed, tipping his hat as he left.

Mary looked at me, her shiny eyes not quite bright enough to hide something that was bothering her. "I understand you are going to be staying out at the Nelsons' place until you are completely recovered." There was an edge to her voice.

"Doc seems to think it will do me good, and I'm inclined to agree with him."

"Oh, I'm sure it will. You've been tied to this room a long time. I just hope you are doing the right thing," she said easily, though I sensed that the notion of me spending time with the Nelsons was somehow behind the apprehension her eyes so poorly hid.

"It's enough to make a fellow downright disagreeable." I grinned at her. "And I wouldn't want to become disagreeable." I don't know why I added that. My brain was already plenty jumbled up where Mary Kenyon was concerned.

Her eyes swept my face, and when she spoke her voice was low, and concerned. "Will you be coming back?"

So, that was it. Suddenly I was feeling hemmed in. While tied to this room, to this bed, when any means of making my own decisions was out of my hands, I had abandoned responsibility to the wind. But now that time was over. I was back in control of my affairs—more or less—and the pressures that went along with it were suddenly flooding over me like torrents through a breached levee. Responsibility! An enemy that has hounded me since the signing at Appomattox Court House when once again I had been given back control over my own affairs.

"I don't know, Mary," I said truthfully. I knew that once away from her care and gentle smile it would be a lot easier to ride off without looking back. I had no good reason not to. Well, maybe there was one, I decided, looking back at her.

She studied my face a moment then opened the basket upon her lap. "I brought you your favorite, darling. Fried chicken, potato salad, and steamed peas."

I watched her unpack the food, painfully aware that if there were words I wanted to say to her, they weren't easily coming to me. I didn't want it to end, yet I knew it couldn't continue.

Seventeen days had done much to complicate the simple life I had nurtured for the last dozen years and grown comfortable with.

11

I CHURNED FITFULLY beneath the sheets that last night at Doc Perry's place; waking, dreaming, seeing dark, faceless strangers lurking at the foot of my bed. Daylight finally drove the haunted shadows from the room and coaxed me awake. I was not well rested, but I was relieved to see the morning just the same. Today was to mark the end of my confinement. I wondered what sort of man Cliff Nelson was. I'd had many visitors over the weeks, but he had not been one of them.

McGee arrived early, his arms full of saddlebags, rifles, and bedrolls. He dumped the gear in a heap at the foot of the bed and announced that he was off to saddle his horse. Perry was coming through the door to see what the commotion was all about and had to step aside as McGee hurried out. He watched after him a moment, then turned a scornful eye at the mess he'd left on the floor. Stepping around it, the doctor checked me over, giving me a clean bill of health.

"Now it is just going to take time," he said, peering at me over his spectacles, "and you not doing anything to exert yourself. I want you to take it easy, and I mean easy."

I promised him I'd not do anything foolish—for a while.

Next, Mary arrived. "Is he decent, Doc?" she asked from the doorway.

Perry waved her in. "He's got his britches on, so I'd say he's decent enough."

She came in carrying that familiar basket and waited as Perry helped me with my shirt, getting my hands and arms into the right holes. "There you go. I'll let you button it up yourself." Perry glanced at Mary. "There, now he is all decent." He smiled. "I'll leave you two alone while he gets his breakfast."

"Thank you, Doc," Mary said.

Perry was a romantic in spite of his cool, professional exterior. We watched the old man limp from the room, then our eyes came together. Mary's face seemed to glow in the morning light, and I wondered if anything that perfect could be real. She looked lovelier than I had remembered.

We looked at each other a long moment. Finally Mary said, "It is a lovely morning for a buggy ride in the mountains. I know the fresh air and the change will do you good, darling, but I will miss you." She took my hand in her slender fingers and gave it a squeeze.

Again, the words I wanted to say evaded me. All I could do was gaze into her deep brown eyes and know that I would miss her too.

"I would like to come out and visit you sometime, if that would be all right?" she asked.

"Of course. I would like that very much."

She looked concerned. "I don't know Verna Nelson at all, and I hardly know her husband, Cliff, except from the few times he has stopped by the café when in town. But I hear they are fine people, and I'm sure they will take good care of you."

I grinned. "If they don't, I'm coming right back here." I was only talking, and she knew it too, but it made her smile just the same. "No one could have taken better care of me than Doc Perry and you. There is no way I can repay you two for that."

"Come back and see us, that is payment enough."

I grimaced. I wanted to tell her I would. Instead, I said, "I don't know, Mary, I just don't know."

She patted my hand understandingly. "At least you didn't say no. I don't want to make you feel obligated to come back. It will be good for you to get away for a while, to have some time to think, to be . . ."

McGee came in grinning. Mary gave him one of her forever smiles and said, "You look bright as a bunny this morning, Mr. McGee."

"Yes, ma'am. I'm looking forward to putting leather between me and my horse." He turned to me. "Got the animals out front, Cap, and I seen Cliff Nelson coming up the street in his buckboard so I reckon you best be getting off your hind end—begging your pardon, ma'am," he amended, giving her a smile.

"Pardon granted, Mr. McGee."

I swung my legs off the bed and sat up. "See? I can move pretty well now," I said.

Marry clapped her hands indulgently. "You are almost good as new."

"Well, not hardly," I said ruefully. "But I'm working at it."

McGee gathered up our gear from the floor and headed out the door with it. Mary said, "Better eat your breakfast now."

She tucked a napkin about my neck. Coming close to me, her perfume filled me with the desire to hold her, to pull her close and kiss her hard . . . but that would only complicate matters. And I wasn't up to that kind of activity yet—at least not physically.

She moved away, leaving me dizzy with desire. "Eat your breakfast, but don't wolf it down. I'll go out front and tell Mr. Nelson that you will be ready to leave shortly." Her voice was strained, but she kept any emotion she might be feeling from her words. She left. Alone again, I tried to put away the struggle I was fighting inside and concentrate on eating.

She helped me to my feet, putting a slim arm around my waist. Having her so close like that only added fuel to the fire burning within me. It had been a long time since I'd been held by a woman, and I'd almost forgotten what those tender creations of God could do to a normally levelheaded man. We made our slow, careful way through the house to the front parlor where McGee and Doc Perry were talking to a man I had not yet met. Perry made the introductions.

Cliff Nelson was a big man who looked like he'd done time in a ring. His wide shoulders and thick arms worried the material of his shirt. Those were the arms of a gandy dancer, I decided, having known more than a few of them in my time. We pumped hands and I noted that although he was no taller than I, he out-strapped me by inches.

The formalities out of the way, Nelson said, "It's a pleasure to meet you, Mr. Kellogg. To tell you the truth, I've been half dreading this moment for weeks." There was a note of apprehension in his voice, and that was understandable, considering the circumstances. After all, it had been his kid who had tried to kill me. I just might be of a mind to take a swing at him for the principle of the matter. Though apprehensive, his friendly smile was genuine. He spoke looking you in the eye and I like that in a man. I liked Cliff Nelson right off. Three weeks in bed had mellowed me some, and I couldn't hold him responsible for what had happened.

Perry said, "Take it easy with him, Cliff. He's still on the mend and has a way to go."

Nelson gave a short laugh. "I won't put him to work hauling gold ore, if that's what you are worried about."

Perry shifted his view and said to me, "I'd like you to stop by in a couple weeks, Mr. Kellogg. Want to give that incision one more look before you head out to Fountain Colony."

"I'll try to do that, Doc." I glanced at Mary, who looked somber. Where was that forever smile now? But I knew the answer.

Nelson said, "Well then, let's get moving. It's a long drive up to the house."

Suddenly the buckboard looked very tall. I eyed it

whimsically and shook my head. "Don't know as I can tackle that yet."

Nelson and Mary gave me a hand up onto the hard seat while McGee tied my animal and the packhorse to the back of the buckboard, then swung up onto his saddle. My saddle, saddlebags, rifle scabbard, and bedroll had been loaded into the back of the wagon. Nelson climbed up onto the seat beside me. Mary stood back, her face tight with concern as Nelson flicked the reins and got the team turned. I looked over my shoulder. Mary and the doctor watched us leave from the front porch of his house.

As we rolled through town, Sheriff Griever stepped out of his front door, gave us a parting wave and watched us leave. In a few minutes, the rough buildings of Calico Lace fell away behind us. Nelson turned the team up a narrow rut that cut back into the tall ponderosa pine trees, and started up the mountainside. The road twisted between tall arching sandstone rocks, shaped by wind and time, then straightened out alongside a fast stream whose headwaters, I imagined, were located somewhere high above timberline, where winter's snow clung to the shadowed places until long into summer.

We continued along the stream, tall pines rising up around us, blocking any sight of the mountain peak, and most of the sunlight. It was cool under those pines, even for August, which had just about run its course by now. For all I knew, it might already be September. Time has a way of slipping by when you've been cooped up for a few weeks.

Nelson cleared his throat and said, "I know apologies

are a mighty poor way to right a wrong, Mr. Kellogg, but I want to offer one anyway. My daughter, Penelda Ann, she's . . . well, she has always been an impulsive girl. Like a two-year-old that has never tasted a bit or felt the sting of a quirt. Her ma and me, we never could decide where she inherited that streak from. Neither Verna nor me is like that." He pulled in a long breath and let it out slowly. "Penelda Ann was real close to her little brother, Joey." Nelson's voice cracked as he spoke his son's name. "When she heard that his murderer was back in town—" The words dropped off. "Well, like I said, she has always been sort of impulsive. I'm sorry it was you who had to pay the price of her impetuous ways."

He fell silent while the creak of the wagon and steady plod of the horse intruded upon the peaceful mountainside. His plain sincerity made it hard to hold grudges. I wasn't even angry with his daughter anymore. The rushing of the stream alongside the road seemed to punctuate the seconds that passed before I said, "Apology accepted, Mr. Nelson. I'd just as soon put the whole unfortunate incident behind us. Sheriff Griever and I hashed over the matter a few days back. I was pretty heated up at the time, but since then I have cooled down. Both Griever and I figure that Penny didn't do anything we would not have considered doing had the tables been turned."

Nelson's face reminded me of chiseled stone with leather hide stretched over it. It didn't move at once, as if he was weighing my words. Then the stone cracked and a smile spread his ruddy cheeks. "My friends just call me Cliff."

"Mine call me Jacob—except for McGee here. He still hasn't got it through his thick Irish skull that we're no longer in the army."

"Now, Cap, be kind to your old first sergeant," McGee complained from behind us. "Tell me, how long have you been in this part of the continent?"

Nelson looked over his shoulder at him. "Verna and me, we come out to the Colorado Territory about twenty years ago. Penelda Ann was four years old, and Joey, he was nearly one. Lawrence, my other son, he wasn't even born yet."

"That's a long time," I said, thinking that I'd never spent twenty years in one place my whole life.

"Yes, it is. There was no town where Calico Lace now sits. That was a place where mountain men and their Ute Indian friends used to get together and spin yarns. But that was a long time ago. Names like Bridger, Carson, Albert Boone, and Grignon were common back then. They used to reminisce upon the old rendezvous and mourn over their demise like it had been the death of a good friend. I met a few of the old-timers when we first got here, but they are all gone now. I suppose a man might find a few of them still up in these mountain, if you looked hard enough, still clinging to the past. There are always those who will hold onto the old ways until death pries it from their cold fingers. But the mountain man is a vanished breed, and so are most of the Indians. How about you two, how long you been out west?"

I shrugged and winced as my skin stretched painfully where Perry had sewed me up. "McGee and I have been moving around with no place in particular in mind since the war. McGee, he's from New York City. I hail from Ohio, but that was a long time ago. We were heading for Fountain Colony when this happened."

"Got a job waiting for you there?"

"No, but McGee and I have done considerable surveying."

"I know. McGee laid out a line for Matt Stringer last week."

McGee piped up. "I told the Cap all about your place."

I said, "We heard that the Denver and Rio Grande was taking on surveyors for a line down to San Luis." I frowned. "But by time we get there General Palmer will have likely hired on all the men he is going to need."

"You won't know until you try," Nelson said.

"Suppose not," I replied, thinking that with fall not far off, work of any kind was likely to dry up.

Nelson gave a flick of the reins and the team perked up, carrying us briskly along beneath the pines. "Verna and I came out here thinking to start up a cattle outfit. We staked our claim to a pretty little valley with nice grass and bought us a starter herd." He looked over and grinned. "And we started losing money right off. I learned, after a few years struggling at it, that I just don't have what it takes to be a cattleman. It was all desire, but desire won't buy a salt lick around here. Somehow we managed to make ends meet, but there was never any profits to speak of. Running a cow camp is a twenty-four-hour-a-day job, Jacob.

"Then a shrewd old businessman up from Texas named Matt Stringer moved into the territory and staked a claim to two hundred sections of grassland just south of my place. Matt had ten times the cow sense as I. He'd grabbed up rich bottom land with good water and tall grass. I'd placed myself in a mountain valley with lots of up and down. That had been my mistake.

"About that time someone discovered gold up at Cherry Creek. My valley was not the place to run cows, but it was the perfect location for a stamping mill. I sold Matt my herd and used the money to build a small mill. This here river we're following runs right through the middle of my valley, and in places drops more than a hundred feet in less than a quarter mile. I had me a source of power to start with and the valley was a natural avenue for the ore wagons coming out of the mountains. Of course, after I got started I had to build me a much bigger mill, and it runs on steam.

"Mines were opening up all over, and some of them producing high-grade ore too, so I was in business, and we've done well for ourselves ever since."

"Sounds like a dream come true," I said, and wondered why some men's lives managed to work their way right even when they made obvious blunders, while others were shattered through no fault of their own. I was feeling sorry for myself, and disgusted with my own self-pity.

"Dream come true?" Nelson's harsh laugh held a bitter edge. "This particular dream is coming up short in two important areas." His naturally easy look had turned to flint. His eyes hardened, and I knew that here was a dangerous man, one I would not want to confront. I'd seen that look before, on the faces of desperate soldiers during long, deadly nights trapped behind enemy lines, or while running a bayonet charge when powder and bullets were spent and all hope for survival was lost. I must have worn that same look one bright June afternoon beneath a telegrapher's staff in the south of Virginia, trembling at the message scribbled hurriedly upon the paper he had just handed me.

In an instant the tempest passed, but in that moment I had learned more about Cliff Nelson than any biographer's pen could have revealed. More than most, I understood what shattered dreams were all about.

"I'd give it all away just to have Joey back," he said heavily, and turned away, staring at the road unfolding ahead, anger draining away like a swollen river rushing to the sea.

"And the second," I asked, curious.

"Oh, it's one of those dreams a man plays with, but know will never happen," he said, once again himself. "I'd like to have me a damned railroad."

"A railroad!" I would have laughed if it didn't hurt so badly. Nelson was grinning too. "You don't want much, do you?" I said.

"I know it is impractical, and practically an impossibility, at least right now. The mines in this area are still small. There isn't enough production to make it economical for a railroad to lay tracks back into these mountains. But a railroad would sure make my work a lot easier. Shipping gold by freighter—both the raw ore and the processed bars—can be a real headache most of the time."

"Have you approached the railroad on the idea of running a spur?"

Nelson shook his head. "We had a town meeting on

the matter about four months ago. The *town* decided it didn't want the influx of people a railroad would bring. One prominent citizen formed a committee that got the people worked up. They killed the idea."

"Griever?" I asked.

"You know?"

"Just a hunch. Matt said the sheriff had some pretty strong feelings along those lines."

Nelson nodded. "He's the one, all right. Managed to get enough votes behind him to bury the issue. That is all fine and dandy for Calico Lace. If they want to remain a wide place in the road, that's fine by me. But in the meantime, I have to hire six or seven guns to ride guard on each wagon I send out. In the last six months I have lost two shipments to a band of highwaymen."

"Two?" McGee gave a long whistle. "That's a bunch of gold to lose."

"Yes it is, Mr. McGee. And the mine owners are none too pleased when it happens. There is talk of shipping the ore all the way to Castle Rock, and if they do, that will put me out of business in a heartbeat. There is a lot of empty countryside between the C-N and Castle Rock, where I have to ship the processed gold. The owners are beginning to think it might be worth the extra expense to carry the ore there themselves, and have it processed at a mill down the line. Highwaymen have no use for a wagon load of rock."

"How long have these holdups been going on?" I asked.

"Not long. They started just after we began processing our amalgam right at the mill. Before that, we shipped the amalgam down south for final processing. In that state, the gold was too bulky to handle, and anyone stealing it would still be faced with the problem of separating the gold from the mercury. This new process makes it easier and more economical for us. Unfortunately, it also makes it easier for thieves to carry it off and spend it. The two shipments we've lost have been big ones, and I can't afford many more losses like that."

An underlying anger colored Nelson's voice, but he kept it under tight control. I wondered if he was really blaming the town, and Sheriff Griever, for his misfortune. We rolled on beneath tall trees, listening to birds and squirrels, and the steady plod of the team up front and our horses behind. The more I thought about it, the more I was in sympathy with Sheriff Griever's attitude, selfish as it might be. The railroads don't pick and choose; they bring in all kinds, both good and bad. When good folks move in, everyone benefits one way or another. But when the bad arrive, the trouble they bring falls on the shoulders of the locally appointed peace officer. Griever wasn't a young man anymore, and he didn't need the extra trouble. He was protecting his interests, and I couldn't fault him for that. But then, I couldn't fault Nelson either.

The road veered away from the stream and began to climb. Presently we came to a broad, treeless slope that stretched away to a ridge line a mile or so off. A chill wind was blowing hard and steady, and Nelson hauled back on the reins and stretched an arm at the windswept plane.

"Tree line," he proclaimed. "You ever been this high?"

"No, never have. Seen it plenty of times, but never had an urge to visit it."

"This here is the highest point between the C-N and Calico Lace. The peak is still several hundred feet above us. My place is down the next valley, a little more than a thousand feet below this point."

McGee drew up alongside us and shivered. "Mighty cold hunk of real estate," he noted.

"That's the high mountains for you," Nelson agreed.

"The road didn't seem so steep as to take us up this high," I said.

"It's deceiving, Jacob, but we've been climbing ever since we left town. In the summer this road is the shortest way into town. But by next month this pass will have snow standing deeper than a horse's bridle. And it will remain clear into May. During the winter we use the valley road. It's eight or nine miles longer, but stays snow-free most of the winter. It winds along the valley floor and eventually runs out onto Iron Ridge land. McGee is familiar with it, aren't you?"

"I say I am. That's the stretch of land I surveyed last week."

"Of course, come winter we don't get into town much anyway." Nelson flicked the reins, and as the team started moving again, I pulled a blanket over my shoulders to cut the wind that bit through my flannel shirt. The iron-rimmed wheels clattered over the rocky pass and soon we were back in the trees. A half hour later the stream swung back alongside the road. Nelson said the water had taken a course through a canyon too narrow for a wagon to negotiate. In a little while trees gave way to a wide, green valley where the fast stream settled down to a slow, meandering ribbon of water, crowded with groves of aspen and cottonwood trees.

The road here was level and smooth, and in the distance appeared a house, nestled snugly into the south side of the valley. We drew nearer to it by the minute, then crossed over the stream on a wooden bridge and pulled to a stop in front of a long log building with a steep roof and a covered porch that stretched across the whole front of it. The logs were hewed square and fit snugly one atop the other with little need for chinking. It had been built to stand against fierce winters, and I suspected this little valley got its share of snow and icy winds come the cold months.

A little way to the right of the main house sat a smaller building with two small windows looking out onto a narrow porch, and beyond, a root cellar of natural stone was built into the side of the hill. Behind us clattered a wind pump, sucking water from the stream to a wooden tank on the hillside above the house. There was a privy, a barn, and corrals strung out haphazardly. I gazed past the barn at the dark smudges that dirtied the intense blue sky far down the valley. Squinting, I could just make out the lines of a tall building beneath the smoke.

"Nice place you have here, Cliff," I said.

A woman appeared at the door, wiping her hands on an apron tied round her waist. She stepped out onto the porch and I swept the hat from my head.

"Verna, this is Mr. Kellogg," Cliff said. "My wife, Verna Mae."

"Pleased to meet you, ma'am," I said.

"Likewise, Mr. Kellogg," she said out of duty, and I had the feeling she wasn't yet sure.

Verna Nelson was a tall woman who showed all the signs of a hard life. Her eyes were green and her smile pleasant, but her face displayed the ravages of too much sun and the cold dry winds of this land. Her hair, carefully folded into a long braid down her back and fastened with a dark ribbon, had begun to gray. She wore a white muslin blouse, with its sleeves buttoned at her wrists, and a gray woolen skirt. In spite of her height, or maybe because of it, she appeared a frail woman. Her narrow shoulders and thin waist stood in sharp contrast to the big man climbing off the buckboard now.

Cliff said, "Verna, tell Lawrence to come out here and carry Jacob's gear into the spare room." He came around the buckboard and said, "Let me help you down off of there." McGee hurried over too, and between the three of us I made landfall without doing any serious damage to Doc Perry's fancy stitchery. With my feet on solid ground again, they helped me up the porch steps.

A towheaded lad of about fourteen rushed out the doorway, then drew up short and fixed his wide eyes upon my face. I had almost forgotten that I looked strikingly like the man who had killed Cliff's son—or Lawrence's brother. The boy's big, round eyes reminded me of it again. I knew the resemblance must be hard on both Cliff and Verna.

"Lawrence!" Cliff snapped. The boy dragged his wide eyes off of me and looked at his father. "Take Mr. Kellogg's gear into the spare room."

"Yes, sir," he said, starting for the back of the buckboard.

Verna held the door open for us as we came through. We entered a long room with open rafters above and a huge rock fireplace against the north wall. Verna hurried ahead of us and arranged small pillows upon a overstuffed armchair.

"Maybe Jacob would like to lie down after the long ride," Cliff suggested to her.

I said, "No, thanks. I've done enough time flat on my back. I'd just as soon sit in that soft chair awhile." I smiled at Verna. "I don't want to feel any more the invalid than I really am." I made my own way to the chair and eased myself into it.

"Can I get you anything, Mr. Kellogg?" Verna asked.

"No, thank you. I am fine."

"Some coffee, perhaps?" she pressed, her natural hospitality winning out over her dismay at my appearance.

"Well, if it is already boiled. I don't want to put you out."

"Nonsense. You aren't putting me out. I know that ride is long and wearisome, and there is a chill in the air." She smiled and headed for her kitchen.

The outside door opened with a kick and Lawrence struggled in, his arms full, McGee tagging along beside him. The boy veered to the left and kicked open another door. McGee came toward us.

"Got the horses put up, Cap. How you feeling?"

"Tired," I said. The strain of the ride was catching up with me.

"Ain't hurting nowheres, are you?"

I laughed. "Nowhere where I didn't already hurt," I said. "But I am feeling weary. Reckon I'm not as fit as I'd like to believe myself to be."

Cliff said, "It might be the elevation here too. We are twenty-five hundred feet above Calico Lace. It takes some getting used to."

McGee said, "Take it easy now. No need to go rushing your recovery."

"Mr. McGee is right. You're welcome to stay here as long as it takes to get you back on your feet."

Verna came from another room with two mugs in her hands. She gave one to me and the other to McGee, and said to him, "How nice to see you again, Mr. McGee."

"Ma'am." He snatched off his hat and tucked it under his arm, taking the cup from Verna. "Pleasure to see you again, and thankya for the coffee."

"You want some coffee too?" she asked Cliff.

"No, thanks. I've got to put the team away. Where is Penelda Ann?"

I caught the frown, though she tried not to let it show. "Penny and that young fellow, Mason, rode down to the mill earlier this morning."

"Mason? What's that man doing here again?"

Verna's thin shoulders shrugged and she let another frown escape her carefully guarded face. "Mason said he wanted to speak to you, Cliff. When I told him you were in town, he and Penny went to the mill to look for Otto."

Cliff huffed. "It wasn't me he come to see. He comes by more than I care for, Verna."

"Now, Cliff," she said lightly, smiling. "I can remember a certain young man who made quite a pest of himself around my papa's farm too."

The hardness softened some and Cliff managed a small smile. "I suppose you are right. Penelda Ann is a grown-up woman now and I reckon I will just have to get used to fellows making excuses to come around visiting. I just wish it was someone other than Mason. He's a shiftless hangabout, and his reputation in town isn't all that sterling." Cliff shook his head, thinking about it, then said, "I need to put the team away. Mr. McGee, we've got a cozy room out back of the barn with a potbelly stove and a feather bed. Bring your gear and I'll show you where it is. We'll be back shortly, Verna."

"I'll have lunch ready when you two get back," I heard Verna reply, but by then my eyes were closed and the chair beneath me was pulling me into its deep softness. My thoughts drifted. I recalled the long ride from Calico Lace, the smell of Mary's perfume, the feel of her arms around my waist, helping me out of Doc's sickroom. Pleasant memories that carried me off to sleep.

12

"MR. KELLOGG . . . ? Mr. Kellogg . . . ?" Her voice reached me from a distance, softly, but urgently.

I opened my eyes. Verna Nelson's face hovered close, and behind her stood Cliff, holding a cup in his hand. I glanced past him to the window. The sky had darkened and deep shadows hugged the porch outside. The odor of burning wood was coming from the fireplace while scattered lamps had been lighted, casting their feeble light about the room. I glanced back at Cliff. His mouth was a tight, worried line across his hard face.

"Mr. Kellogg?"

I shifted my view.

"You have slept away the afternoon. You must be starved," she said. "I've fixed something for you to eat."

I nodded and straightened up in the soft chair. Verna went back to her kitchen while Cliff stared out through narrowed lids, taking a sip of coffee. Suddenly his forehead furrowed worriedly and he turned abruptly on his heels and strode to the darkening window. McGee, I noticed, was hunkered down by the fireplace, feeding logs into the flames that warmed the room. He stood, slapped the ashes from his hands, and came over.

"Feeling some better, Cap?"

Cliff's back was toward me. I inclined my head at him and gave McGee a questioning look.

"Family trouble," he whispered, frowning.

"Penny?"

He nodded.

I grimaced, thinking I understood the worries a father might be having right about now. "She hasn't come home?" I asked softly.

"Been gone all day."

Just then Verna emerged from the kitchen, carrying a tray. She arranged dinner on a table by the chair and said distractedly, "If there is anything else you want . . . ?"

"This is just fine, Mrs. Nelson."

She gave a quick smile that faded as she paused to study her husband. She stood there a moment, chewing her lower lip, then returned to her kitchen. Verna Nelson, I noted, carried her height well. She seemed not to be burdened with self-consciousness, as some women are who stand taller than the average. She was proud of her height, and she moved with grace. Harsh mountain winters, parched winds, and a burning sun may have stolen some of her outward beauty, but they never laid a finger upon that inner elegance that radiated from this woman.

McGee went back to nourishing the fire, leaving me

to nourish myself. Cliff brooded at the darkening sky a long time. When he did turn around, worry was in his eyes. He stepped away from the window.

"You have any children, Jacob?"

I shook my head.

"They can be worrisome at times," he said and headed toward the kitchen. McGee was watching me. When I looked over, he gave a wan smile and returned his attention to the fire.

I worked at my dinner, trying not to make Cliff's problems mine. I felt better when I had finished, and told Verna so when she collected the dirty dishes.

Cliff came from one of the bedrooms carrying a rifle. He tugged his hat over his head and said, "I'm going out to look for them, Verna."

"Want some company?" McGee offered.

"No, thanks. I can handle this alone."

Verna went to him and put her hand upon his thick arm. "What are you going to do?" she asked worriedly.

"Find them."

"Don't be too hard on her, Cliff. At least hear them out before you do anything."

"I'll be fair."

"I know you will."

The door latch lifted and both Verna and Cliff turned.

"Penny!" Verna said.

Cliff remained silent, his view hard and fixed upon his daughter. Penny closed the door and looked at them. Just as I remembered her, she was a tall, striking girl—more than a girl—a woman, and I wondered why she had not married yet. Her long gray skirt was smudged and dirty now after her ride, yet she stood straight with her shoulders square and a determined set to her strong jaw. Penny had inherited her mother's height, and her pride. Verna started for her, but Cliff put out a hand and stopped her.

"Where have you been, Penelda Ann?" he demanded.

Her eyes hardened. "Out," she said flatly.

"Out? Out where? The mill?"

Penny nodded.

"To see Otto?"

She nodded again.

"All day?" he snapped.

She lifted her chin and stared her father in the eye. "No, not all day. I went for a ride afterwards."

"You were with that Mason character, weren't you?"

Penny tossed an accusing look at her mother, then glared back. "Yes, I went riding with Mason. Is there a crime in that?"

Cliff sucked in a long breath. "Where did you go?"

"Nowhere. Just followed the river for a while, then came back. I lost track of the time. When we started back it was already getting dark." Her face softened. "We just rode. Rode and talked, that's all."

Cliff let go of his anger and Verna went to her daughter, draping a protective wing over her shoulder. "Let's get you some dinner, dear." They started for the kitchen. Cliff said, "What did Mason want to talk to Otto about?"

Penny looked back. "He was interested in hearing more about that new method you brought back with you from the Black Hawk Mill. The one Nathaniel Hill figured out."

Cliff looked surprised. "The Hill Process? What did he want to know about that for?"

Penny shrugged and sighed. "I don't know. Mason is interested in a lot of things about mining." Her mouth dipped into a pout. It was a pretty pout, I thought. "Sometimes I think he is more interested in the mill than in me."

Cliff cleared his throat and said, "We have guests, Penelda Ann."

She had not realized we had been there all along. Her face reddened, then her eyes fixed upon me.

"This is Mr. Kellogg, Penelda Ann."

"Yes, I know." Her voice was suddenly quiet.

"Miss Nelson," I said and struggled to sit a little bit straighter in the chair.

She hesitated, then left her mother's side and advanced cautiously toward me. Maybe she was afraid I was going to spring for her throat. Little did she know that was not a concern. Just the same, she stopped four feet away, her eyes fixed upon mine.

"I . . . I, ah . . . I don't know what to say," she began awkwardly, her voice not much above a whisper. "I am so sorry . . ." Her head shook as she spoke and suddenly her eyes filled. "I thank God every night that you are still alive. It was a horrible injustice and I'm so very sorry."

Impulsive. That was the word her father had used. Perhaps it was true; it must have been to some extent. But he didn't mention that Penny was also a sincere, caring person. The remorse I saw on her face told me more now than anyone else had so far.

What could I say after that? It wasn't all right, of course, but I told her so anyway.

"It's not all right," she insisted. "It was a terrible mistake . . ."

"That's what it was." I cut her off. "A mistake, and we all make them." I was amazed at the philosophical bent my thinking seemed to have taken during my convalescence.

Penny wiped a tear from her cheek. "Thank you, Mr. Kellogg," she managed to say and turned so that I wouldn't see her crying. She and Verna left the room, and Cliff came over.

"This has been real hard on her, Jacob." He gave a small grin. "Not that it has been any picnic for you, either."

"I can see that."

"It's a lesson I hope Penelda Ann will never forget."

"She won't," I said. "A person who doesn't learn and grow from their mistakes is a fool, and I can tell that Penny is no fool." There I was, philosophizing again.

"Thank you, Jacob, for seeing that in her. No, she is no fool, but she is impetuous, I'm afraid. What happened was a disgrace, and I guess we are all looking for your forgiveness. What with the death of Joey, we had just begun to pull our lives back together. Then this happened. They say the Good Lord gives each of us trials," he mused. "These last six months have surely shown us ours."

"Well, bad luck can't last forever."

"Hell, I know that." He had become somber, and I could see he was not a man to dwell on the misfortunes of life. "I've some fine sipping brandy," he went on, casting off his moodiness. "You up to having a drink?"

McGee was suddenly there. Nelson laughed and said, "You won't let me drink by myself, will you, Mr. McGee?"

"My sainted mother, God rest her soul, taught me manners fittin' a gentleman, she did. And one of them was to never let a friend drink alone."

I laughed gently because it hurt too much to do the job right, and said I'd join him. He half filled three small snifters and passed them around. Presently a warm glow settled about the room, and in a little while Verna and Lawrence joined us. The fire was warm and comfortable and I was growing weary again. Mainly because I was not doing anything, I suspected. We talked of mining and surveying, of railroads and politics—Calico Lace politics, and somewhere along the way I nodded off to sleep.

McGee woke me some hours later. The big living room was deserted and the lamps turned down. He said everyone had gone off to bed, and bed was where I belonged too. I could see no reason to argue that and let him help me into my room.

The week passed uneventfully, except that I grew stronger. McGee remained faithfully at my side, keeping me company, taking me on short walks around the grounds or along the river. He managed to come up with a couple of fishing poles from somewhere and we found us a nice deep hole beneath the bridge where a big, olive brown cutthroat trout hid out.

I felt sorry for McGee, being tied down by my slow recovery, but he didn't seem to mind. I was feeling stronger after that first week, and in a few more weeks knew I'd be well enough to leave. Though he did not mention it, McGee was itching to move too.

Another lazy week slipped by, then one day while down at our favorite fishing hole feeding worms to that cagey old fish, McGee said, "You know, Cap, we could make Fountain Colony in two days. You're about fit to ride, I'd judge. Maybe we ought to be thinking about moving on."

I threaded another worm onto my hook and dropped the line into the water, letting it drift over that dark hole where that cutthroat was lurking, waiting to finish lunch. "I've been thinking some on that, McGee," I said, playing the line just so to attract that fish's attention. "We can just ride over to Castle Rock and take the train to the Colony."

McGee thought that was a good plan. "How long you figure you are going to want to stay here?"

I gave a short laugh. Laughing no longer hurt. "Until I catch this wily critter."

McGee grinned. "In that case, maybe we should just file a claim on this here patch of grass."

"Very funny." I flicked the pole, making the line jerk in the water. "We are well into September, and you know how fast winters come on in the high country. I want to be away from here before the snow flies."

"I'm thinking another week or two, or we are liable to spend the winter here."

"That's the way I figure it too." I felt a tug and snapped the pole. An empty hook cleared the water and that old fish had himself another worm. McGee was making a remark about running out of worms when we heard the clatter of a buckboard coming up behind us.

Cliff reined the animals to a stop. "I've been after that crafty old monster for years. I wish you better luck than I've had."

"We've fed it about every available worm in this here valley," McGee lamented.

Nelson smiled. "That's why I finally gave up on him." He paused, eyeing our worm can and giving a small laugh. "I'm riding out to the mill. Care to come along?"

I'd never seen a stamping mill before and said I'd be pleased to join him. McGee had already been out to it. He said he had shaken hands with the devil once and had no desire to get reacquainted. He was going to stay and take another shot at that trout. His meaning went over my head, but Cliff wore an amused smiled as I climbed up into the seat next to him. He toed off the brake and we rolled across the bridge.

At a fork in the road, he bore to the left onto a rutted lane that had seen a lot of heavy traffic. It was the freight road from the mines, he told me, as he flicked the reins and the team picked up their gait. A little way off a small herd of cows were grazing, moving lazily up the valley; all that was left now of Cliff's ranching endeavors.

In a few minutes the plume of black smoke down in the valley loomed nearer, the building there slowly growing larger and more impressive. The road crossed and re-crossed the river three times and finally angled along the valley's southern slope. Drawing closer, I saw that the stamping mill was actually made up of three different buildings, all connected by long, covered walkways. Even before we arrived, the racket of the milling operation could be heard reverberating up the valley. Cliff brought the team to a halt in front of the largest building and climbed down.

The mill was a tall clapboard affair, freshly painted a bright red with the name "THE VERNA MAE MILL" painted in white above a wide door. North of this main structure sat a low, one-story clapboard building with three black iron chimneys sticking up through its roof. The chimneys were busy belching black smoke that hung above the valley in a dark cloud. This boiler house was connected to the main building by means of a covered walkway. Above the slanted roof of the main building stood the third structure. It was a tall, narrow edifice with three rows of windows, the third and lowest row standing just above the slanting roof of the main mill building. At the very top of the complex was a gaping doorway large enough to hold two Baldwin locomotives side by side. A curving trestle swung away from the door on spindly timbers and marched clear to the valley wall, and tiny ore carts were making their way back and forth along it.

"I was lucky to find a vein of coal on my land," Cliff said, seeing me wonder at the activity way up there. "That's why I chose this spot to build my second mill. The first was about three miles up the valley where there was a waterfall to power it."

"Most impressive. I'd like to see more."

A short, round man with a bald head and snow white muttonchop whiskers came from the building, puffing on a long-stemmed clay pipe. *"Guten morgen, Herr Nelson,"* the fellow called out, above the din of the place.

"Good morning, Otto," Cliff shouted. "Otto, this is Mr. Kellogg. I told you about him. Jacob, Otto Wagner." Nelson pronounced the *W* as if it were a *V*.

Otto stuck out a plump hand and told me he was very pleased to meet me.

Cliff said, "I brought Otto here to help me set up this mill. He came straight from the steel factories of the Ruhr Valley in Germany, and he knows his stuff."

We entered the cavernous mill, where the rumbling of the heavy machinery instantly drowned out our voices. A flight of stairs took us up to a walkway running high overhead. If anything, the pounding was even louder up here, while from one level below came the hiss of escaping steam that reminded me of a riverboat with its valve cocks wide open. Nelson pointed across at the huge hammers creating a never-ending earthquake. One after another they would rise and fall, rise and fall, in their earth-shaking dance.

"Those are the stamps." He turned, and now I could see where freight wagons entered the mill and dumped their loads of ore from the mines down a chute that directed it to the stamps. Cliff's finger moved and pointed at something on a lower level.

"Those are the vanners," he shouted. "Nothing more than a series of screens that sift the crushed rock. They help to separate the lead from the silver and gold. We don't get much silver in this area, not like they do up around Leadville."

The racket tortured my ears and my head began to pound in time with the stamps. We started along the narrow walkway and dropped down another flight of stairs. The pounding diminished a trifle, replaced by that hissing of steam which was even louder down here.

"After the ore is sifted, it comes here, is mixed with mercury, and cooked for eight hours." His arm swept along a line of twelve huge, iron-lidded vats. Sweat was pouring off me from the heat of the place, and the racket had set my teeth a rattling. "That is called amalgamating," he shouted near my ear. "Afterwards, the slurry is transferred to settling tanks. The gold is then separated from the mercury and melted down into ingots . . . there, in that room."

We left the mill with my ears ringing, and the mountain air slapped my burning cheeks when we finally emerged from the hellish place. Nelson saw my discomfort and gave me a grin. "I try not to spend too much time in there. I've been told that years of working in a stamping mill makes some men go deaf. Isn't that right, Otto?"

"*Ja, ja.* No more hear." Otto tapped his ears and smiled. They were both shouting, even out here.

Cliff said, "Otto and I have to go over the details of the next shipment, Jacob. Excuse us, and feel free to wander wherever you want, only keep clear of the overhead trestle. It's a sixty-foot drop, and it's not uncommon for someone to accidentally drop a chunk of coal from up there."

They went into a small building a few hundred feet

from the mill, and I drifted over to the stream because it seemed a peaceful place, and a safe distance from that rumbling building I'd just escaped. But even here the ground beneath my boots still shook with each drop of those huge iron hammers. I knew why McGee had shown little interest in coming here twice.

I sat against a tree and tossed a handful of pebbles into the rushing water. The sun was warm and felt good. I noted a freight wagon making its slow way along the road, drawn by eight mules and loaded down with rock—gold ore, I reckoned. Time dragged by.

I got bored just sitting, and surveying the property, I began to wonder about a little shed near the building Cliff and Otto were in. It looked somewhat like a carriage house, only the door was wider and taller, and was reinforced with iron bands and wore a stout padlock. Unlike the other buildings about, this one was built of stone. My curiosity piqued, and with nothing but time on my hands, I wandered over for a closer look. It was indeed a sturdily built shed with only one door and a small window set high in a wall.

The glass was dingy. When I pressed my face to it, I saw the wagon locked up inside there. But not like any wagon I had ever seen before. It was more like an iron box on wheels; eight or ten feet long, six feet high, and four feet wide. It had been constructed of plates riveted together, and was entered from the back through a single iron door. It didn't take a lot of imagination to figure out how this odd conveyance was used, or the purpose of the narrow slits cut into the plates all around the box. This was how Cliff Nelson shipped his gold to the railway at Castle Rock.

I backed away from the window, into something cold and hard poking me in my spine.

"Turn around real slow, mister," a voice from behind ordered. I went rigid and spread my hands to show I wasn't armed. Then I was staring down the tunnel of a Sharps 50. The hammer was all the way back on full cock and a beady eye squinted over the rear sight. A finger was curled through the guard and gently caressed the trigger.

"Take it easy with that thing," I said, lifting my arms. I hadn't heard him come up behind me, and that irked just a little. A month ago it would have never happened.

He backed away a step and waved the rifle at the closed door. "In there. Move it!"

"All right, all right," I said quickly, not wanting to rile him any. I scudded sideways, my back still against the brick wall. It connected to the clapboard building, and then I was at the door.

"Open it," he ordered.

Slowly I put my hand to the knob and turned it. The door swung open and I backed inside, my arms still reaching.

Otto and Cliff came around, startled at first, then Cliff's eyes narrowed and he barked, "What the hell is this all about, Hank?"

"I seen this stranger sneaking about the wagon shed, Boss. He was peeping through the window at that new wagon. What with all the trouble we've had, I figured—"

"Put that rifle up," Cliff snapped, not waiting for him to finish. "This man isn't a spy! He's my guest!"

"Guest?" Hank blinked, turned a confused eye at me, then quickly lowered the rifle. "I'm . . . I'm real sorry, Mr. Nelson. But I ain't never seen him afore, and I was just carrying out your orders."

"All right, just get out of here," Cliff said impatiently.

The mill guard apologized and started to back out the door.

Cliff frowned. "Hold on there, Hank."

"Sir?"

"I'm sorry I jumped on you like that. You were just doing your job, and you did it well. It's just that we are already responsible for shooting Mr. Kellogg once. I don't want to see the same mistake happen again."

Hank's eyes brightened a bit. "Oh, you're *that* fellow." Apparently the story of Penny's impulsiveness had made its way through Cliff's employees. Cliff looked embarrassed. Hank went on quickly, "I wasn't planning on really shooting him, Mr. Nelson. Leastwise not unless it was necessary," he said and left.

Cliff looked over, frowning. "Jacob, I'm sorry about that."

"It was my fault. I should not have been sticking my nose where it didn't belong."

"Nonsense. I gave you run of the place. Everyone has been strung up tight the last few months. The holdups, you understand. Many more of them and I'll lose this business, and my men all know that. I should have realized Hank would be on the lookout for unfamiliar faces." He indicated a chair.

"You're looking tired. Sit for a while. Otto and I are almost finished here."

I wasn't tired. I had regained much of my strength in the couple weeks I'd been in the valley, but I obliged him just the same. I had only just sat down when a knock sounded at the door and another man came in.

"Hello, Boss," a medium-height man in the dusty clothes of a mill worker began. "Just wanted to let you know that we've got all the—" He saw me sitting there and went suddenly silent, a concerned look leaping to his face.

"It's all right, Larry. Mr. Kellogg is a friend."

"Kellogg? Say, you that fellow that Penny . . ." He glanced suddenly at Cliff, his cheeks reddening some. "Err, what I mean to say is you're that fellow that Penny mistook for John Carver, aren't you?"

"That's right," I said, trying not to grin.

"I'm pleased you are up on your feet again," he added quickly.

"What did you want, Larry?"

"Oh." He looked back at his boss. "Those special ingots you told me to pour. They are all finished. Butterworth, he's trying to round up some gold-colored paint right now."

"Good, good. Let me know when Butterworth is finished with them."

"Right. When you going to be needing them?"

"Figure sometime next week. Thursday or Friday."

"They will be ready for you." Larry looked back. "Nice to meet you, Mr. Kellogg," he said and left.

"Larry Higgins. The mill's foreman," Cliff explained briefly.

"I thought Otto here was in charge," I said.

The plump German chuckled. "*Nein.* I just build it

and keep it from falling down. Don't run it. I am a craftsman, *ja*!" He struck a match and put it to the bowl of his pipe.

Cliff grinned. "Any more questions, Otto?"

"Nein."

"Good." Cliff closed a thick book on the desk in front of him and stood. "I will be by in the morning to see how things are going." Otto took the chair behind the desk as we started out. But Cliff stopped and looked back. "Otto. Has that fellow Mason been hanging around the mill lately?"

"Mason? *Ja, gestern.*"

"Yesterday? Does he stop by often?"

"Ja."

Cliff frowned. "The next time he shows up, have Hank run him off. I've a bad feeling about that one."

"Ja. I will tell Hank."

"Thanks."

We left Otto sitting there puffing his pipe, returned to the buckboard, and headed back to the house.

13

VERNA NELSON SET out dinner plates from a stack on her arm, making her way around the table. She came to a certain place, paused, and stared longingly at the empty chair. There was the look of deep sadness in her eyes. I'd known that very same glassy-eyed stare myself, gazing at the burned-out hulk of a farmhouse back in Ohio so many years ago. I could even dredge up those old feelings now, if I made half an effort. I didn't. I'd been back over that barren ground too many times to count.

I watched her from that too comfortable chair in the living room near the fireplace. Her teeth gnawed at her lips a moment, then she drew in a sudden breath and continued on around the table, setting out plates. After the silverware and water glasses were in place, Verna glanced up, found her youngest sitting on the hearth reading a tattered copy of *Harper's Weekly,* and said, "Lawrence, go fetch Mr. McGee and your sister."

The boy frowned and reluctantly set his magazine

down. "Hold there, Lawrence," I said, "let me get them. The walk will do me good." I had spent most the afternoon after my trip to the mill in that fat chair, and I was feeling fat myself. I wanted to get out and stretch my legs before nightfall stole the rest of the day.

"Sure thing, Mr. Kellogg," he said, grateful to be left to his reading.

"Thank you, Jacob," Verna said from the table, where she was checking over her handiwork. "Penny had her horse out earlier. You will likely find her in the barn brushing him down."

The afternoon had worn thin and now the sun was slanting toward the far side of the mountains. A warm, clean smell was in the air, and for some reason it reminded me of Mary Kenyon. I don't know why, but she was suddenly very near and real in my thoughts. I stepped off the porch and angled across the wide stretch of open ground toward the barn and corrals. I remembered her arms about me when she had helped me out of Doc Perry's house the last time we were together. It had been almost a month since I had seen Mary, and I realized I was missing her. I crossed to the barn and let the memories fade. I would see her again before I left for Fountain Colony. I'd return to Calico Lace at least once—to drop in on Doc Perry, and Mary.

I circled the barn to the back door and heard McGee snoring beyond. I went inside and said, "Wake up, you lazy good-for-nothing. Light is still in the sky and dinner is on the table." I plucked his hat off his eyes.

McGee snorted and parted one eye. "Cap? What? What time is it?"

"Supper is waiting. It's time to pull your lazy bones out of that bed."

He sat up and swung his legs to the floor, scrubbing the sleep from his eyes, yawning and stretching hard enough to make his spine crackle. "Where did the afternoon go?" he asked, yawning again.

"Apparently you slept it away."

"Reckon I did," he agreed, taking his hat from me and smashing it to his head.

"Did you ever catch him?"

He blinked, sleepy-eyed. "Catch who?"

"That old Jonah-eater under the bridge, that's who."

"Oh, him. That critter's got more hook savvy than any other fish I've ever seen."

I grinned. "Well, there is always tomorrow. Verna wanted me to call Penny too. Have you seen her around?"

"I ain't seen nothing all afternoon but the inside of my eyelids."

McGee and I went around to the front of the barn. No Penny. Only the usual number of horses in the stalls . . . minus one. The sky was darkening when we stepped outside again and scanned the valley. Then McGee pointed at something. In a moment I picked them out too. A pair of figures on horseback. They weren't moving, which is why they blended with the trees there so well.

"There she be," McGee said.

They were too far to be seen clearly, but it appeared they were just sitting there talking. I considered taking one of the horses and fetching her home, but just then the two parted. Penny turned homeward while the other rider, a man, reined about and started off toward the mill. As he rode away to the east, the last dying rays of sunlight slanting low along the valley fell upon him. Something flashed back the light. I saw the glint only for a few moments before the sun fell below the tree-tops and shadows began flooding the land.

Penny turned into the corral and I took the reins from her as she dismounted.

"Your mother is waiting dinner on you," I said, turning the reins around a rail.

"I'll be there in a few minutes. I want to brush her down first," she said, working the cinch buckles and hauling the saddle into the barn. She returned with a bucket of brushes and combs, and began yanking a comb through the matted hair along the horse's back. I took a brush and started working on the legs.

McGee said, "I'll go ahead and tell Mrs. Nelson you two are putting away the horse." He folded himself through the rails and started for the house.

"I don't like putting her away for the night without brushing her down," she said, tugging the comb through the knots. "After all, I wouldn't want to go to bed with first combing my hair," she added with a smile. Then she gave a smirk. "Sometimes I treat these animals like they were people. I'm a little crazy that way."

"Everyone is crazy some way," I said. "Take me, for instance. I'm just crazy about trains. I love to watch them rumbling by, like fire-breathing dragons. I could sit alongside a lonely stretch of track for hours, just waiting for one of those black, puffing monsters to arrive, pulling all those cars behind it. I love to see a big locomotive puffing and hissing up a grade, its black smoke rising to the clouds. Or feeling the rush of steam warm your face and hands as one of those iron monsters rumbles past you, shaking the very ground beneath your feet—a little like your pa's stamping mill?" I grinned. "Yep, I'm a little crazy that way."

"I like trains too," she said. "I like seeing all the faces pressed against the windows and wondering where those people are going."

"They are going all over the country," I said. "It wasn't so long ago a trip to California would take months in a prairie schooner, and there was only about a fifty-fifty chance you'd make it alive, and with any of your belongings intact. Now folks make the trip in comfort, crossing from one ocean to the other in only weeks."

"The railroads are changing the look of this nation," she noted, "bringing new towns and commerce with them."

"That they are. They are good at what they do . . . sometimes too good. Sometimes I think they are bringing too many people out where they don't belong."

Penny frowned. "Now you are beginning to sound like Thad Griever."

I laughed. "I hope I'm not that gloomy. But I'll wager a time is coming when a man won't be able to ride twenty miles without stumbling across some new town that has sprung up just because the railroad came through."

"Is that all bad? It's a big country," she said, looking at me across the back of the animal, her blue eyes wide and wondering. She had her mother's face and build, but the sun and wind had not yet had enough time to work their damage on her. Looking at her, I realized that, although young, she was no child. I knew she was close to twenty-five, a ripe old age to still be living at home, unmarried. I wondered why. But it was not a question I would ever ask her. As I watched her combing out the knots, I thought of Betty. Betty had had a special love of animals too. I saw that same affection in Penny's eyes now, and then it occurred to me. Betty was only eighteen when the twins were born, and before she was twenty-two, she was dead. Looking at Penny, I found it hard to believe she was already three years older than Betty had lived.

There were other similarities too. Her stubbornness, her temper . . . her sincerity. I was suddenly uncomfortable looking at her and glanced away at the darkening sky. "It gets dark quickly in this valley," I said.

"Pa says we have what the old-timers used to call 'Indian Nights.' "

"Indian Nights? What's that?"

"That's when the darkness comes on you so quickly, it takes you by surprise. Like an Indian in a forest. The sun will be shining one minute, then the next minute it's dark. Indian Night, that what they used to call it, or so Pa says. But I think he just made up the story for us kids when we were little."

"It's a good story, and a good name. You ever have any dealing with the Indians around these parts?"

"Oh, some," she said, working on the horse's long, black mane, "but nothing serious. The only Indians around here are the Utes, and as long as I have known them they have been friendly toward us. When we were working cattle they would run off a few head every year. Then Pa went and talked to their chief about it, a queer fellow by the name of Ouray. They struck a deal where we'd trade cows for blankets and other such things that didn't amount to much money-wise, but kept things friendly on both sides." Penny thought a moment, remembering, then laughed.

"You've never met an Indian quite like Ouray. Seems he took to the white man ways like a duck to water. He served imported wine and Cuban cigars whenever a guest would come calling at his tepee. I remember a story Pa told about the time he and Joey went to visit Ouray . . ."

She stopped with sadness suddenly welling in her eyes. "I can't seem to go five minutes without thinking about him," she sniffed, dragging a finger over the tear that streaked her cheek.

I grimaced. "It takes a long time for something like that to heal. I know."

She frowned, unwrapped the reins from the rail, and took the horse and her bucket of brushes into the barn. She reappeared a few moments later, brushing her hands against her skirt. Her mood had turned stormy. "We better be getting back to the house," she said curtly and scuffed away. I watched her go up the porch steps and into the house, I shut the gate and made my own slow way back. Penny had taken Joey's death hardest, and the wound was going to take a long time to heal—like another fellow I knew. I put the thought out of my head. I'd healed enough over the last dozen years where I could at least do that much.

The family and McGee were sitting around the table

when I finally came through the door. An uneasy quiet had filled the room, and I took my chair.

Verna said to Penny, "Did you have a nice ride, dear?"

"Uh-huh," she replied, pushing the food around her plate with her fork.

Verna and Cliff exchanged glances. Apparently they were familiar with this taciturn side of their daughter. Cliff cleared his throat and said, "Jacob and I rode down to the mill this morning. Henry thought Jacob was spying on that new wagon and nearly blew his head off with that big Sharps he totes around with him."

"Oh, how dreadful," Verna said.

"Yes, ma'am," I interjected, grinning. "I thought so too." I looked at Cliff. "You figure all that armor plating will keep your gold safe from those highwaymen?"

He shook his head. "No, I don't. At least not in the obvious way." He paused. "And in a certain respect, yes. I'm counting on it to keep the next shipment safe."

That pretty much told me nothing. Cliff and Verna exchanged looks again. Cliff went on, "You see, we have held back making any large shipments since that last holdup. The bulk of what we have refined is safely in the vault, but we need to move it soon. There is no cash flow when the gold just sits there."

McGee looked confused; I know I was. "Care to run that past me one more time?" he asked. "I lost you somewhere between 'no, it ain't gonna help, and yes, it is.' "

Cliff leaned back in his chair and started from the beginning, marking the points with his fork as he went along. "I'm not so thick in the head to think that two thousand pounds of armor plating is going to stop someone from holding us up, if they have a mind to do so," he began in a deliberate manner. "But what I am hoping is that everyone else will think I am. Most will agree that an armored wagon is the obvious way to haul something of great value. So, hopefully, when it rolls next week there won't be any question in any-one's mind that it is loaded to the gunnels with gold."

"Sounds like you built yourself a rolling advertise-ment just asking to be robbed," I said.

He thought over what I had said, slowly nodding his head. "You might say that. But of course, I don't want anyone to take it, or even make an attempt. That wagon cost me plenty to build, and men might get killed. But I'd rather they take it, and the lead ingots it will be carrying, than the real shipment."

"Lead?" I asked, getting a glimmer of what he was planning.

"Painted gold, of course," he explained. "The real shipment will be sent out in the buckboard, by a dif-ferent route."

It wasn't exactly a novel idea, but the plan had merit. "You are hoping no one will suspect a lone, unescorted buckboard, and instead go after a heavily guarded ar-mored wagon."

"Wouldn't you, Jacob?"

"I suppose so," I said thoughtfully, "if I was a high-wayman. One thing I've been wondering about. How does word get around when a shipment is supposed to go out?"

"That wouldn't be hard to find out. We ship twice a

month. Anyone watching the mill could pretty much figure out when we are preparing to take another load down to Castle Rock. That's not what bothers me." He glanced up sharply. "What bothers me is how they seem to know when we have a big shipment, or a small one. Like I said, we've made several small shipments the last few months. Not a one of them has been bothered."

"Inside help."

"We've thought of that," Verna said, "but there aren't any suspects. All our people have been with us a long time. We've never had a reason to suspect any of them."

"It's a big puzzle," Cliff said. "Thad Griever hasn't been able to turn up anything either. That is why we are handling this shipment differently. We've kept it hushed up. Just Otto and Larry know what we are really up to, and I trust both those men implicitly."

"McGee and I now know your plan," I reminded him.

Cliff grinned. "Then, if the wagon gets held up, I'll have me two prime suspects now, won't I?"

"Cliff!" Verna gasped.

"I'm only funning, Verna."

"I certainly hope so. That is a terrible thing to say to guests under our roof."

We had picked our plates clean by then—all except Penny, who had hardly touched her food. Verna began clearing away the dishes while McGee and I took ourselves over to the fireplace and hitched a couple chairs closer to the heat. The nights were getting colder and the first snows would be on us soon. In a little while

Cliff joined up with three snifters and a decanter, and filled each with a measure of brandy.

"This will help warm our insides while the fire works on our outsides."

McGee raised a toast to him, his family, and his fine home. We drank to that and made some small talk about the weather. But I could tell there was something more on his mind. Suddenly he shifted his chair around to face us and leaned forward, his face taking on the look of a man about to talk business.

"What are your plans now?" he asked us.

McGee chuckled and said he was planning to try for that elusive fish again in the morning.

Cliff smiled briefly then fixed his expression along more somber lines. "I mean further on down the road."

"That's about as further as I care to plan right now," McGee came back glibly, already feeling the brandy.

But there was a reason behind the question, I could tell, and I said, "We'd like to be on the move before winter sets in and the snow comes. McGee and I talked some about it this morning. Maybe next week. I'm fit enough to take to a saddle again, and the longer we delay here, the harder it will be to find work. Not much to do for men like us come winter."

"Still aiming for Fountain Colony? You know, they have pretty mild winters down that way."

"It's as good a place as any, and maybe General Palmer is still taking on surveyors for that little railroad of his. I hear he intends to push track clean through the Rocky Mountains, and maybe even as far south as Mexico."

"You know he has already laid steel down from Denver?"

"We know. Down to the Colony and beyond to Pueblo. He may already be as far as Walsenburg for all I know."

"I've been shipping gold to Denver on the D&RGW since Palmer opened the line. Tracks run through Castle Rock, you know."

"Yep, we know that too," McGee said. "Cap and me were thinking of catching the train in Castle Rock and riding it down to Fountain Colony. That way we figured it would save Cap some hard riding and give him a mite more time on the healing side."

The look that came to Cliff's eyes made me squirm. They had brightened suddenly with McGee's words. He said, "That sounds like a good idea, McGee. And I've another for you two gentlemen to consider."

I tried not to frown, but I didn't like what I'd heard in his voice. I thought I knew what it was too, and I asked, "Could it be you want us to ride along with you in the buckboard when you make that big gold shipment?"

Cliff tasted his brandy, watching me over the rim of the glass. "No need to look so worried, Jacob," he said. "After all, it will be a lot easier on you riding in the buckboard than the back of a horse."

"But a lot more dangerous, especially if your little deception happens to leak out," I replied.

He made a wry smile. "*If* it leaks out. I don't think it will. But I'd feel a whole lot easier having a couple guns along—inconspicuously—just in case. The clever part of doing it this way is, it won't look out of place.

We'll just pass the word that I'm driving you to Castle Rock to catch the train. It's the truth, and everyone will know why. The whole town knows how badly you were hurt. No one will think it strange you leaving in the buckboard rather than straddling a horse."

"Won't two wagons going to the same place look suspicious?" I asked.

He dismissed my suggestion with a wave of his hand. "No, not at all. We always send the gold by way of the valley road. The grades are less and it's a more open route. I'll just send the armored wagon out in the morning. We'll start for the pass later. It's shorter that way, and the route we would naturally take, not wanting to jostle you around any more than we have to."

It sounded as if he had given this plan some considerable thought. I wondered how long he had been thinking of enlisting me in his deception. Could he have been planning it like this all along? I didn't hardly see how that was possible. He had no way of knowing we'd be considering taking the train once we left here. Still, I found it curious.

The offer was worth considering, but I still wasn't one hundred percent convinced the security around the mill was all that solid. Maybe Verna believed all her employees were loyal and honest, but that didn't make it so. I wasn't prepared to rush ahead and put my neck on the line just on her word—at least not tonight. If I had wanted to do that, I'd have stayed in the army, where a man gets paid for his foolishness. I'd have stayed in Ohio, if I'd had half a backbone left inside me. I dismissed that thought. Barren ground, I reminded myself.

"Well?" Cliff prompted.

I glanced over at McGee. "It's up to you, Cap," he said, looking up from his brandy.

It was always up to me. McGee had found the perfect retreat from life in me. I made all the decisions. Normally, I didn't think about it much, but tonight, for some reason, it irked me.

"You don't have to give me an answer tonight, Jacob. Sleep on it."

Indecision. I was beginning to hate what I had become. My sudden irritation with McGee, I knew, was only misdirected anger at myself. *Indecision.* It was a part of me now, and it was up to me to change it if I didn't like it.

"I'll sleep on it," I agreed.

"Good. That's all I can ask. Now, can I interest either of you two in a game of poker?"

"I'll go a couple hands," McGee said.

I threw back the rest of my drink, feeling the brandy burn all the way down. "No, thanks," I said, standing. "I think I'll step outside for some air." I wanted to be alone with my thoughts.

Verna's voice reached me from the kitchen. "Better put on a jacket, Jacob. The evening air has got a nip to it tonight."

I stepped into my room, and as I took my coat from the hook, I eyed my saddlebags hanging beside it. For some reason I opened the flap and lifted out the holster. Pale moonlight through the window shown dully off the handle of the revolver. I grimaced, drew it from the leather, and looked at it. I couldn't remember the last time I had shot it, or even worn it. Had it been eight

months . . . a year . . . ? I had been good with it once—
very good. A man had died because of that, and even
though he had deserved to die, that never made the
memory of it any easier.

I put the revolver away, but couldn't put it out of
my mind.

14

I LEANED AGAINST the porch post and watched the moonlight glint off the rippling water below. From up here the stream looked like a river of beaten silver. A cool breeze stroked my face, and it felt good. Down upon the quiet bottoms a few head of cattle grazed, spread out along the water. Probably the same cows I'd seen earlier. Cliff only kept a few head these days, more a hobby to him that any source of income. Judging from the milling operation I'd seen today, Cliff didn't need the income. Overhead, the blue-black sky was crazy with stars; so many that they washed across the heavens like sugar frosting on a birthday cake. It was the kind of display you only see in the high mountains.

Dark shapes darted low in the sky, drawing my eye. Bats. Not quite mice and not quite birds, I mused, yet they seemed to do just fine for themselves. They never worried about who they were or what they were becoming. I grinned. Introspection was becoming a bad habit . . . and sometimes a dangerous habit, when it distracted the brain and dulled the senses.

I didn't hear her there, had no idea how long she had been watching from the shadows at the far end of the porch, until her voice stirred me from my reverie.

"Indian nights," she said quietly, stepping into the light from a window, pulling the shawl more tightly about her shoulders. She stopped by the rail and looked at me. Her eyes said she wanted to talk. Then she gazed out across the valley, past the river.

"When I was a little girl, Pa and I would come out here at night and we'd play a game of make-believe. See that big rock across the river? That would become a bear. And those three trees over there? They were the Indians hunting the bear. See how they appear like men crouching?" She gave a short laugh. "They don't look much like it now. The moon has to be just right, and they were a lot smaller trees when Pa would tell the stories." She paused, remembering. "But when he did, this whole valley turned into a magical kingdom; all alive with strange and funny and wonderful creatures that he would conjure up for us kids out of his imagination."

"Sounds like a pretty good way to grow up," I said. "You were fortunate to have a father who took the time to be with his kids. Not everyone had that."

"It was a good way to grow up," she agreed, her words low and thoughtful. "The trouble is, he hasn't let go of those little kids. I'm all grown up now, but he still treats me like a child."

"A woman your age usually has herself a husband and two or three kids by this time."

I could sense her stiffen at my side. "Go ahead and say it," she answered sharply. "Others do, behind my back. Old maid. That's what a woman's called who is nearly twenty-five and not married and still at home."

"That wasn't what I was thinking."

She grabbed the shawl tighter in her fist. "It's not like there is much opportunity to meet anyone, living way out here. And when I do, Pa always finds something wrong with him." She let her anger flow easily, like her laugh. Penny Nelson did not try to bury her feelings. It was an honest quality. Admirable perhaps, but one that left a person terribly vulnerable.

"You are talking about Mason?"

Penny nodded, staring out into the night. "I don't know why Pa doesn't like him. He hardly knows him."

"Maybe it's not him."

"What do you mean?"

"Not long ago you mother and father buried a son. You buried a brother. Losing a child is a horrible thing. I'm thinking they are not ready to lose another—even if she is all grown up."

"You think that's why Pa's so against me seeing Mason? He's afraid I'll find someone to marry and then he will have lost me too?"

"That could very well be the reason."

"That's not fair."

"Maybe not," I agreed. "How long have you known him?"

"Almost five months."

"Has the subject come up?"

"You mean marriage? Not really, not in so many

words. But a woman's got a feeling for these things. I know he's thinking of it."

"Hum. Marriage is a lifelong journey. You hitch yourself to the wrong man, and that journey can be pure hell. When I was twenty I didn't think about it much, but now I'm nearly doubled that, and age gives a person the advantage of hindsight."

"You're making yourself sound ancient. You're not that old."

"The years don't matter as much as the amount of living that's been squeezed into them."

She studied me with wide, curious eyes, and I had that funny feeling again, like I did earlier in the corral, when she had told me about the "Indian nights."

"And you have done a lot of living?" Penny asked. There was none of the earlier friction in her voice.

I grinned. "Sometimes I wondered how I ever fit it all in."

"Were you ever married?"

My breath quickened, like it always did when I thought of the past—of Betty, but this time it was different somehow. I found it easy to talk about. Maybe it was because I was finding Penny easy to talk to— once we had gotten past our rocky beginning. Like me, there was an emptiness inside her. We were much alike; two people looking for a way to fill a void. I told her about the war, and about Betty and the twins. I gave her the short version of how McGee and I had gone west, right up until the day we rode into Calico Lace. Her face tensed up and I ended the tale. I knew what she was thinking; she was feeling bad enough about the mistake without me bringing it up again. When I had finished I knew we'd forged an understanding between us that hadn't been there before.

Penny thought about it and said. "You loved her dearly, didn't you?"

"Yes, I did," I managed to say and stared into the darkness and nodded. A lump formed in my throat right then, and there really wasn't much more to add anyway. I don't know if I moved, or she had, but suddenly we were standing much closer. Her shawl brushed my shoulder when she turned to peer at the ribbon of moonlight down below and her hand was upon the railing, close to mine. I felt funny, like I hadn't felt for years. It had been a mighty long time since I'd stood in the quiet of an evening with a pretty woman at my side, looking at the stars. Too long.

She said, "I suppose I have no right feeling sorry for myself. I forget how hard the world can really be."

The lump melted and I brought the conversation back around to Mason. "You'll find someone, Penny. That's just the natural course of things. Some people just take longer than others, and maybe that's because they have set their sights a mite higher than all the rest." I grinned. "But don't let your age force you into something that might be wrong for you. Make sure you know the man you will marry—really know him."

Penny, I was learning, was as changeable as mountain weather. That had been the wrong thing to say to her. Suddenly her mood turned and her mouth tightened as her eyes raked my face. "I should think I'd know a person well enough after five months."

I looked away from her and studied the big "bear"

rock across the river. "Was that Mason you were riding with this evening?"

"I don't have to discuss my personal life with you," she answered.

"You are the one who brought it up."

"I never!" Her eyes shot up at me, narrowing in the moonlight. "Why would I volunteer to discuss my personal life with you?"

It was a good question, and it had occurred to me too, but I didn't want to argue the point. "I retract the question, Penny. You don't have to answer it if you don't want to."

"Of course I don't have to answer it," she retorted. She glanced away, her tone softening. "It was Mason. So what?"

"So nothing. I don't care who you keep company with. You're not my kid."

"I'm not a kid!" she shot back.

"I stand corrected."

Penny jerked the shawl and snapped her head around, flinging her long curls along her shoulder. There was the faint hint of perfume, and it was a very grown-up odor. It reminded me of Mary—different certainly, but I so seldom encountered the stuff that it easily brought back memories of the last time. As I stood there, I was aware of the growing desire to see her again. I remember her telling me that getting away would do me good. She had been right.

"You are suddenly awfully quiet."

"I'm not in the habit of speaking to the back of people's heads. Beside, I got the distinct impression that the conversation was over."

She turned back and peered into my face. Her eyes had softened and she said, "I'm sorry, Mr. Kellogg. I guess I'm not in a very good mood tonight. Pa says I'm temperamental. I'll argue with him that I'm not, but inside, I know it's true. I'm sort of extra sensitive when it comes to Mason. Pa doesn't like him, but I'm sure that's just because he doesn't know him."

Something in that made me uneasy. I didn't know why at first, but then I remembered that Julie had said just about the same words trying to defend her boyfriend, John Carver. How much of what Penny said did she really believe, and how much was plain infatuation?

"Cliff doesn't strike me as a man who passes judgment without having some very good reasons."

"His only reason is that Mason is in love with me, and that doesn't strike me as being very fair." Her eyes flashed. "Do you know that Father left orders with Otto that Mason was to be run off the next time he shows his face at the mill?"

"I was there. The way I heard it, Mason is beginning to make a pest of himself. Can't hardly blame your father, what with the plans he's making for that special wagon and the next gold shipment. He doesn't want word of the switch leaking out."

Something changed in Penny's eyes. There was a twitch that came and went in an instant, and left a nagging suspicion in my brain. I studied her, watching her lips draw together into a hard line.

"What are you staring at?"

"He *doesn't* know, does he, about the switch, I mean?"

"Of course not!" She glared accusingly. "You don't trust him either. You're just like Pa. Mason is a good, kind man, and his only crime is that he loves Cliff Nelson's daughter. You know why he's making a *pest* of himself around the mill? It's because he wants to become a mining engineer. And I'll bet Pa doesn't know that. Mason wants to go to that new School of Mines in Golden and get proper learning about mining." She whirled away, folding her arms across her chest and drawing in a sharp breath. Without looking back she said, "And when he goes, I'm going with him."

Stillness settled upon the porch, except for her rapid breathing. There was the obvious question that needed asking, and after turning it over some in my head I realized there just was no delicate way to say it. "Has he asked you to come with him?"

Her breath caught and her shoulders quivered slightly beneath the shawl. She was crying and she didn't want me to see. All at once she rushed down the steps and out across the dark land. At the river's edge she stopped and stood there, staring across at the bear rock.

The door opened behind me. I heard Verna's footsteps come up beside me. "I didn't mean to overhear."

"She has a lot to sort out."

"Yes. Since Joey died, we all do. It has been hard adjusting." Verna watched Penny standing down by the water.

"She'll adjust."

"Of course she will, Mr. Kellogg. We all do. You adjust or you die . . . or worse."

I grimaced at the truth in her words. But in what direction does that adjusting take us? The answer to that question is what I have been searching for since the war ended so many years and endless miles ago.

15

NAGGING THOUGHTS KEPT me tossing and turning through the night, and when first light touched the curtains, turning them pink with the dawn, I came full awake and lay upon my pillow listening to a blue jay scolding outside my window. The household was still asleep, all except for Verna, who was quietly rattling pans in the kitchen.

I swung out of bed and dressed. Then I stood by my saddlebags, considering. Finally I reached inside for the holster belt. Seeing it the night before had kindled something inside of me. Images of the revolver had haunted my dreams. I sat on the edge of the bed and looked at the piece in the growing light. It was a short-barreled .44–40, one of Colt's new Army Models. Although not old, it had been well used at one time, and showed it on the barrel and cylinder, where the finish had been worn by sliding it in and out of the leather. The action was smoother than when it had come from the factory, since I'd worked it some with a hard stone, then practiced until I had become proficient enough to kill a man in a fair fight.

I had carried a revolver during the war, an old cap-and-ball .44, and I had killed with it too. But somehow, killing for your country felt different. Pondering on it, I couldn't say why that should be. It had happened in Brownsville, and after they buried the tinhorn, who hadn't been very lucky at cards either, I'd packed the revolver away. That had been over a year ago. A drifter, I had decided, can get by with a good saddle carbine. In the years McGee and I have been riding together, my '66 Winchester has served just fine.

Now, as I studied the revolver in the light of this new day, I had a feeling that the time had come to bring it out again and brush up on what I might have forgotten. It was loaded. I could hear the rounds shaking in their chambers, see their five dull gray heads peeking out the cylinder. The hammer was down on an empty chamber; the safest way I knew to carry it loaded.

I slipped the gun back into its holster and slung it over my shoulder. Verna gave me a smile as I crossed the parlor and she said, "Morning, Jacob. You're up early. Care for some coffee?"

"Yes, ma'am, I would indeed."

She glanced at the holster. "You expecting trouble to come knocking at the door?"

I dropped the holster onto the table and lowered myself in a chair. "The coffee smells good," I said. She was wearing a flour-splashed apron, and when she poured the coffee the odor of freshly kneaded bread was strong.

"Thank you, Mrs. Nelson." I took the cup. "No, I'm

not expecting trouble. Thought I'd get some practice in. It's been a long time since I've fired that thing."

"Practice?" she asked, her eyebrows arching slightly. She tried not to act surprised, or pleased. I couldn't read what she was thinking.

"If I take Cliff up on his offer to ride shotgun to Castle Rock, I'd like to be sure I can still hit what I aim at." That was part of the truth, but there was something else. Something that had troubled me after watching Penny's friend, Mason, ride away the evening before, just ahead of the shadows sweeping across the valley as the sun dipped below the mountains—Penny's Indian night.

She smiled again. "Then you must be feeling very well."

"That I am." I sipped the coffee while Verna went back to the counter and removed a tea towel from the rising bread dough in a bowl. "Where would be a good place for me to burn some powder? I don't want to disturb you or Cliff."

Verna turned, wiping her hands on the apron. "There is a place up the river about a quarter mile. A stand of aspen trees along the road to Calico Lace. There is a clearing and if you shoot up valley there isn't anything there you need to be concerned about hitting." She paused, the glow fading from her face, and when she continued there was a heaviness in her voice. "It's where Joey used to go, whenever he wanted to do some shooting."

She just stood there, looking, and I wondered if perhaps she wasn't seeing John Carver in my face. Again, I couldn't read that look. She turned abruptly and began punching down the dough that had risen up over the rim of the bowl. I finished my coffee and left her there taking out her anger and frustrations on the breakfast biscuits.

Around behind the barn I reached for the door then stopped, withdrawing my hand from the knob. McGee was probably still asleep, and I wanted to be alone, anyway, to sort through the thoughts that kept nagging at me. I saddled my horse and climbed stiffly onto his back. A slight twinge reminded me I was using muscles weak from disuse, and not completely recovered from Doc Perry's scalpel. It was the first time in nearly a month I had ridden, and that long since my animal had had anyone on his back. I suspected he might be frisky, and maybe even a bit balky. I didn't want to be bucked so I kept a tight rein as I started away from the corrals.

The ride was jarring at first, until I found the rhythm. As I started up the road, Cliff's offer to drive me to Castle Rock in the buckboard began to look more and more appealing. But in a few minutes I got the hang of it—after a fashion—and developed a technique that allowed for acceptable progress at the expense of minimal pain. Nonetheless, after about ten minutes of this I was relieved when the stand of aspens Verna told me about came into view on my left.

I took a sigh of relief when once again solid ground was beneath my boots, led my horse down to the river, slipped on a halter and tied it off to a young aspen. There was plenty of green grass in the bottoms and water in reach. He'd be happy as a hog in a rainstorm. I strolled off a few hundred feet looking for something suitable to shoot at. It didn't take much searching. In the middle of the clearing was a tree stump riddled with holes. Glass shards and shattered crockery littered the ground all around it. I bent stiffly for a spent .44 casing. Joey had stood on this very spot, learning the character of his gun, not realizing he was practicing for his own death. The ground was littered with empty cartridges. I grimaced, looking around. He had spent a considerable time learning how to die.

A little searching turned up chunks of glass large enough to be shot at again. Among the litter were two whiskey bottles missing their necks. I arranged them upon the stump and paced off five long strides. The revolver slid from my holster in a slow, mechanical fashion. There was nothing fancy, nothing quick about it. I was out of practice, but more than that, the movement bit deeply into my chest. The healing muscles weren't used to the motion. My first shot went wide, kicking up some dirt three or four feet to the left. I had to go back to basics.

Spreading my feet shoulder width, I turned slightly, cocked the revolver, steadied it, caught my breath, and gently squeezed the trigger. The .44 boomed and bucked, and the whiskey bottle shattered into a dozen pieces. That's better. I repeated the whole procedure, splintering the second bottle. A dozen shots later I had my eye back, and the Colt was beginning to feel more at home in my fist.

An hour later I had progressed to clearing leather smoothly and placing a bullet generally where I intended it to go. No precision shooting here, but enough competence to hit a man-size target at fifteen feet. My draw was still slow, and part of that was because of the wound still healing, but being fast wasn't what was important. Plenty of duelers have died trying to be fast. It was the sure, steady hand that usually won out.

I'd made progress, and that was good enough. I'd gone through a box and a half of shells and my ears were pounding, the muscles across my chest aching. The chambers filled with fresh rounds, I slipped the gun into the holster and was about to return to my horse when the hairs at the back of my neck suddenly stiffened. I was not alone out here. Somewhere hidden eyes were watching me, probing my back like fingers in my spine. Shoulders tense, I tuned slowly, hand hanging near the worn walnut grip of the Colt.

She moved out from the trees, gathering up her skirts as she came through the tall grass. "Jacob." Her voice was light and cheerful, and there was that forever smile.

"Mary!" I cranked my jaw and shut my mouth. "I didn't hear you."

"I'm not surprised," she said, coming near. "With all that shooting I am amazed you can hear anything at all." She glanced at the revolver, a frown marring the pretty smile. It passed and she said, "You are looking fit, Jacob. I am delighted to see you doing so well. Verna Nelson's cooking must agree with you."

I reached out and took her hands. It seemed such a natural thing to do. She said, "You don't mind that I came out to see you, do you, darling?"

The endearment sounded a bit strained, but just then it was pleasant to the ear. That same perfume that I remembered sweetened the air, and her hair bounced lively about her shoulders when she moved her head, unbounded by the ribbon that customarily held it back in place. As those wide, brown eyes sparkled and search my face, I wondered how I could ever mind her coming to visit. "You look lovely, Mary."

She blinked and said, "Thank you, Jacob. I am glad you think so."

I fought the urge to hold her, to pull her to me and kiss her hard. I was shocked to realize how much I had missed this woman. I shifted my eyes off her soft face, hoping my desires were not as plain as I feared they might be. Wipe that silly grin off your face, I told myself. You haven't had a schoolboy's crush in almost twenty years.

"Did you ride out alone?" I asked, seeing her buggy waiting on the side of the road through the trees.

"Julie is watching the café. It was a nice ride. Early mornings are beautiful, don't you think?"

They were, especially when someone like Mary was suddenly there to share one with you. I didn't tell her that. Instead, I grabbed that old crutch when words were difficult to find. "There is a nip in the air. I smell snow."

She laughed. "How does anyone *smell* snow?"

"The same way you smell danger, I reckon."

"That's just an expression," she said as we started down toward the stream to collect my horse. My hand found her waist. She didn't resist, but moved a little closer.

"How have the Nelsons been treating you?"

"Like the king of England has come for a visit."

She laughed again. "That well? You might never want to leave."

"They are fine people, Mary. But they've come onto some hard times."

She nodded. "Yes, I know. First their son is killed, then their gold shipments are stolen." Mary sighed. "No one ever said life was easy. There are the good times and then the bad."

I winced, bending to untie the rope. "Yep, that pretty much sums up the days of man on this green earth."

On the way up to her buggy, Mary asked, "Does Cliff Nelson have any idea who is responsible?"

"For the stolen gold?"

She nodded.

"It is a mystery to him. He believes all his employees are loyal, but there must be someone on the inside passing out information."

Mary frowned. "That *is* a mystery. And he does not suspect anyone?"

"No."

"Interesting."

"You think so?" I paused to look at Mary.

"Yes, don't you?"

"It's interesting, if you like to worry over puzzles."

"Do you worry over puzzles, Jacob?"

"Sometimes."

"This one?"

I had to grin at her inquisitiveness. "I have to admit, I've been turning it over in my head, some, trying to figure it out. I agree with Cliff. Someone on the inside is giving out information."

Her eyes widened while her voice lowered. "What have you figured out?" she asked. "Do you know who is responsible?"

I laughed. "Who do I look like? Allan Pinkerton?" I handed Mary up into the buggy and tied my horse behind it. The ride back to the house was a pleasure compared to the ride out—for more reasons than just the easy sway of the buggy. Mary had brought new sunshine into the valley. Her wide, forever smile warmed me, though it didn't dispel a sudden chill when I remembered that Cliff's problems might become mine, if I took up his offer.

"Miss Kenyon," Cliff declared coming out onto the porch when we pulled up. "How good to see you. What brings you out here?" Then he looked at me and gave a short laugh. "Well, I reckon I can guess the answer to my own question. Here, let me help you." He hurried to the buggy.

"Thank you, Mr. Nelson," she said, accepting his arm and placing a foot lightly upon the iron step-down. I swung off the other side and came around as Mary was brushing the dust from her gray skirt, looking around at the large house and outbuilding. "What a lovely place you have here. It's just as nice as Thad said it would be."

"Did you have trouble finding us?"

"Not at all. Thad drew me a map. Once I found the turnoff, it was just a matter of following the road all the way."

"Come on inside." Cliff started up the steps. The door opened and Verna stepped outside.

"Verna, dear. Mary Kenyon. She drove out to visit with Jacob."

"Hello, Mrs. Nelson. I have seen you in town, but I

don't believe we have ever met." Mary offered her
hand, but Verna's remained folded against her apron.

"No, I don't believe we have," she said coolly. "How
nice to meet you."

Mary's hand fell slowly to her side. "Yes." She
glanced briefly at me. A smile flickered to life, then
died.

Cliff cleared his throat and said, "Why don't we all
go inside for a cup of coffee? Mary must be tired from
the ride."

Tension thickened. "I could use a cup of coffee," I
said, taking Mary by the arm. Verna's coolness was a
surprise to all of us. She turned stiffly and led the way
into the house. I guided Mary inside while behind us
Cliff took up the rear, shaking his head.

Lawrence looked up from his breakfast and smiled.
"Hello, Miss Kenyon," he said.

"Hello . . ."

"Lawrence," Cliff said.

"Oh, yes. Lawrence. You have eaten at the café with
your pa."

"Yes, ma'am," he replied.

"Miss Kenyon has come all the way out here to visit
with Mr. Kellogg."

The boy went back to his biscuits and eggs. Verna
went into the kitchen for coffee and Mary gave me a
questioning look. I shrugged. I didn't understand
Verna's coolness any more than she.

Cliff led us into the parlor and offered Mary a chair.
Verna brought the cups in on a tray and passed them
around, offering cream and sugar, and taking a seat
next to her husband on the settee.

"Tell me, Mary, how was the road?" Cliff asked, attempting to chip away at the ice.

"Clear, but cold," she said. "Especially above timberline. But still no sign of snow. Otherwise, it was a pleasant ride." Mary sipped the coffee and set the cup back upon its saucer. She looked at me. "You were out on horseback, Jacob. Does that mean you are well enough to ride . . . to leave?"

I gave a laugh. "I was on horseback, it is true. But I wouldn't exactly call it riding. More like holding onto the red end of branding iron, trying not to get burned."

Cliff said, "Jacob has made great strides. You'd hardly know he was teetering between here and the hereafter only a month ago."

Verna looked up with flint in her eyes. "Jacob has been a very agreeable guest," she said flatly, her voice empty of any expression. The two women's gazes locked, then disengaged, Mary forcing a wan smile to her lips that she extinguished with another sip of coffee.

"I have had good care," I added. The conversation was taking a dead-end trail. The honey-thick tension brought out strain lines on Mary's forehead, and a hard, scrutinizing gaze in Verna's eyes. It was like the electricity in the air at a cockfight, just before the birds were dropped into the ring. I suspected the genesis of Verna's coolness, but felt it was misdirected. I ached for Mary's discomfort at this arctic reception. She certainly had not expected it. I could sympathize with both ladies, but my loyalties were being pulled toward Mary.

Cliff saw it too. "Jacob, I'll bet Mary would like to take a tour of the place," he said, pretending not to notice the storm brewing in his parlor. "With that warm sunshine, it seems a shame to stay under a roof. Why don't you show her around? Take her down to the mill. It's quite a sight, Miss Kenyon."

"Yes, I'd like that, Jacob," she agreed quickly. "That is if you feel up to it." Her cup clinked upon the saucer and she set it on the low table.

"Of course I feel up to it," I declared, eager to put breathing room between the two of them. "I'm about as spry as a yearling colt." At that moment I'd have been *up to it* even if I had one foot in the grave, holding onto the short end of a bear-greased rope. I took her hand and helped her to her feet.

Verna remained absolutely silent, something deep and brooding smoldering in her eyes. She didn't say good-bye, didn't even smile. Dutifully, Cliff remained at his wife's side.

Outside, we stood a moment looking out across the grass to the river below. Mary lifted her face toward me and rolled her eyes. "I'm so sorry I came out here, Jacob. I never expected Verna to react to me like that . . . I just don't understand." She guarded her voice so that her words would not carry past the door. I grimaced, not knowing what to say, and guided her down to the buggy.

"Well, I for one am glad you came, Mary." That brought a smile to her face. "I don't understand it either. If I had to guess, I'd say that in some vague way Verna has connected you with John Carver."

"Me?"

"He did work for you, and still comes into town to see Julie. Everyone knows it."

"But I didn't have anything to do with it," she retorted indignantly, flashing eyes suddenly narrowing. "Verna has no right blaming me for her son's own stupidity."

The harshness of her words stunned me. *Stupidity?*

Mary realized what she had said, saw the look of dismay leap to my face. She stammered and tried to cover over the callous remark. "Well, I mean, it was pretty stupid to go up against a man like John Carver. Everyone knew his reputation with a gun. Don't you think so too?"

Her face was cheery again, but I couldn't forget that dark look that had passed like a cloud over it. I helped her up onto the buggy seat and turned the horse away from the house. McGee came around the corner of the barn and waved us to a stop.

"Miss Kenyon, it's mighty nice to see you again," he said, coming over. "What are you doing here?"

"And you too, Mr. McGee," she said. Her mood had switched tracks without a pause and she was once again her lovable self, forever smile and all. I frowned. Hiding my feelings so cleverly was a skill I had never mastered very well. I was much like Penny in that way. Mary seemed to have it down with a well-practiced ease. "I drove out to see how Jacob was mending."

"He's about all mended. We'll be pulling out of this here valley pretty soon," he said with a wide grin.

I flicked the reins and got the horse moving before he said any more.

"See you when you get back!" he called.

We crossed the bridge, taking the road toward the mill. Mary straightened around in the seat beside me and tugged her bonnet down more securely, then pulled on a pair of thin, black leather gloves.

"Jacob, you're scowling. Don't be angry with me, darling." A pout briefly crossed her pretty lips. "I didn't intend to sound cruel. It is just that I don't like being blamed for something I didn't do. I didn't shoot her Joey."

She sounded sincere, but an underlying hardness came through in her words and I wondered what she really thought.

16

THE MORNING GAVE way to hot noon sun, but clouds were gathering on the horizon, gray and ominous, and I kept one eye on them while the other delighted on Mary Kenyon. She seemed a different person than the one who had taken bitterly to Verna's coolness. She was her old self. The sweet and vivacious Mary I remembered from that morning in the café. It seemed so long ago now. So much had happened to me in between.

Mary's anger had evaporated with the morning chill, and when I tried to recall her stormy eyes, it was like trying to remember a dream—unreal and easily forgotten. We had stopped briefly at the mill and Otto had come out to give us his jolly greeting and offer to show Mary around. She was impressed with the size, but disturbed by the racket of the heavy stamps rising and falling and shaking the earth. She'd taken my arm when Otto wasn't looking and whispered in my ear, "Let's leave this dreadful place."

That was over an hour ago, and now, as the buggy moved slowly along the ridge road toward the eastern spill of the valley, the morning's unpleasantness was far removed. The sky ahead of us was clear and blue and warm. But behind us the gray clouds kept pushing over the mountains, banking up high above the valley, above Cliff's homestead.

"What a beautiful view," she said, peering out at the endless eastern plains that stretched clear to the Kansas border and beyond. "Let's stop for a while, Jacob. I've brought a picnic lunch and I'm starving."

I hauled back on the reins and the buggy creaked to a halt. Mary dropped lightly to the ground, placed her hands upon the curve of her hips, and surveyed the broad, flat slice of land that spread out beyond the mouth of the valley. Matt Stringer's Iron Ridge outfit. She turned slowly, scanning the fringe of trees to the north and then the plume of black smoke rising off the valley floor far to the west.

A frown soured her face. "That is awful. I am certainly glad we can't see all that dirty smoke from Calico Lace." She came back to the buggy. "We can have our picnic right here."

Ahead of us the road began to drop quickly out of the valley, down through pillars of wind-carved sandstone. The tall pines of the mountains were all behind us, having given way to the scrub oak and short juniper of the foothills. Farther out, even those petered out to the tall grass of Matt Stringer's land. "Mighty pretty view, Mary. Stringer's land is fine country for growing cows."

"Yes, it is," Mary agreed, lifting that familiar wicker

basket from under the seat. I climbed out of the buggy, not nearly as lightly and gracefully as she had, and quite pleased just to be alive and well enough to get out under my own power.

"Darling, come sit down." Mary patted the ground near a cloth she had spread out, arranging the contents of the basket upon it.

"How do you suppose a man like Cliff Nelson could come out here with cattle ranching in mind, and pick a place in the mountains to do it when there was all that fine grass out there for the taking?"

Mary made a face. "To tell you the truth, Jacob, I don't think Cliff Nelson was cut out to operate a cow camp. Come, sit down, you make me nervous standing there."

"No, I don't suppose he was. He admitted as much himself. He came out here and saw the beauty of this place, and just sort of forgot that cows have to have something to eat, and a place to spend the winter." I lowered myself on the spot she was indicating.

"Cliff Nelson is a romantic," Mary observed, her voice telling me that she had no real interest in this line of conversation. She busied herself setting out bowls of food, plates and linen napkins. There was potato salad, fried chicken, cantaloupe, and a bottle of delicious-looking red wine. Carefully she unwrapped two crystal wineglasses from a towel that she had tucked safely away in the corner of the basket.

"Millford had some stored in a back room," she explained, seeing my surprise.

"You had a picnic in mind when you came up."

"I was hoping we might have some time to get away

by ourselves," she said with a pretty smile.

She handed me a corkscrew and asked me to do the honors. I twisted out the cork and filled both glasses, then held mine to the sunlight, watching the tiny bubbles rising to the top, catching the light.

"Do you know how long it has been since I've had a glass of wine?"

"How long?" she asked, moving closer. Her perfume was suddenly heavy in the warm air. I looked away and tasted the wine.

"A very long time . . . and this is excellent. Not that I know anything about wine, you understand."

"What's to know? You either like it or you don't."

I was absorbed by her beauty. I realized that I was staring.

"What's wrong?" she asked innocently.

"Nothing," I said too quickly. "I'm . . . I'm just really hungry."

"I think I have everything we need to satisfy you," she replied, wearing a funny smile, handing me a plate. "I fried the chicken just for you. I remembered it was your favorite." She glanced at the empty glass in my hand. "My, you drank that quickly. You do like wine, I see." Her voice held a bit of playful banter. "Let me fill it again."

Afterward, she took a sip from her glass and set it carefully upon a small saucer so that it wouldn't tip on the uneven ground. She took a small bite of her chicken, her wide, brown eyes watching me. I may have been out of practice some, but I knew straightaway what she was up to, and I had no problem playing along with it. I was flattered she wanted to flirt with me. I liked her, and plainly she held similar feelings. But I just wasn't used to females batting their eyes and coming on so boldly. Women didn't do that unless they meant business, and for some reason, I knew that Mary was only playing the game. She was teasing. It was just a game to her. That was all right too. I could play along as good as the next guy.

There was much about this woman I did not understand. So many inconsistencies that kept cropping up. I was learning that with Mary, you could never be sure what she was feeling. She seemed to be always trying to keep you slightly off balance.

I wondered how far she was going to carry this, and decided to take matters into my own hands. I stared into her face a moment then said, "Each time I see you, Mary, you look more lovely . . . more desirable." Then in an intensely obvious way I let my eyes roam, and linger in a most forward fashion. When my view had finally traveled back to her face, she was blushing.

"Why, Jacob, what a nice thing to say," she replied smoothly, not so easily flustered as I thought she might be.

"It is true, and you have been so kind to me. I'm thinking it is time to take our relationship to a new level," I laid on the charm as thick as I could muster for being out of practice as I was.

Her eyelashes fluttered then dipped toward the wineglass. Was she just a little confused by my sudden change from shy and retiring to aggressive? The pursued becoming the pursuer?

"I don't know what to say, Jacob."

"Don't say anything. Just let me look at you. Just

think, you and I are probably the only two people within miles of here . . . all alone, together," I said, putting a lecherous inflection on that last word.

"Why, Jacob, you're a romantic too. I would have never guessed," she breathed, patting her lips with a crisp, white napkin.

"A beautiful woman can make a romantic out of any man, Mary." I placed my hand upon hers and leaned closer. A shudder ran up her arm and she withdrew her hand under the pretense of reaching for the wine bottle.

Teasing didn't come natural to me, like it does for some men, but after I started it, I had to admit I was enjoying the game. Mary appeared at a loss as to what had come over me, and I rather suspect she was wondering if the fish she had caught was more than she could handle. Like that big lunker under the bridge. I wanted to laugh, and to break off the game, and tell her how obvious her flirting had been, but like Colonel Harrison had once told me, when the enemy turns and runs, that's when you mount your forces. Not that I could ever picture this lovely creature looking so distraught now as an enemy. But in some vague and fuzzy way, I figured the principle applied.

"You haven't touched your food, Jacob," she noted distractedly, refilling both our glasses. Liquid fortitude? I wondered.

"Suddenly, I am not very hungry." I was starving!

Her eyes flashed across my face and settled out somewhere across the valley. "My, I feel a chill in the air." She crossed her arms.

"Snow is coming. Remember, I told you this morning."

"Yes, you said you could smell it."

"But I'm not feeling cold now, Mary," I said with as much passion as I could muster. It must have been too much for her. She sprang to her feet and went for a shawl in the buggy.

"There, that's better," she said, pulling it over her shoulders and clutching it tightly in front of her.

I almost burst out in a laugh, but held it back, guarding the smile that was shoving at my lips. Victory. Mary's flirtatious advances ceased and she was distracted the rest of the picnic, eating quickly. When she made a stab at a different line, something neutral and unromantic, I couldn't contain myself.

"You did that on purpose," she scolded when I'd finally stopped laughing.

"I was only playing your game, Mary."

"My game. Why, I never!" She began packing away the picnic, practically throwing the dishes and bowls into the basket. When I tried to help, she said, "It is getting late. If I'm to be driving back to town this afternoon, we had better be getting back to the house."

I noted that the word *darling* was distinctly absent. "I'm sorry," I said. "But you started it."

"I surely do not know what you are talking about, Jacob. I think that hat must be feeling rather tight now."

It wasn't as though I didn't want her. I did, but without the schoolgirl games.

"I said I was sorry."

She took the basket to the buggy and climbed aboard without waiting for me to hand her up.

"All right, we'll go back."

"Thank you," she replied curtly.

I turned the animals' noses toward the thick, gray clouds spilling over the peak, working their way down the valley. The air *had* turned chilly now. I glanced over at Mary still wrapped in her shawl. "I don't like the looks of those." The clouds were disturbing enough, but not as much as trying to discover the true nature of the lovely woman frowning on the seat beside me. Where was that forever smile now?

We didn't talk much, and what little there was of it kept to neutral grounds: the scenery, the weather, a bird she didn't recognize, a bear that watched us from up the side of a hill. The skies above the house were dark and gloomy, heavy with moisture. The temperature had plunged and once the clouds let loose with all that moisture, it was bound to come as snow. Cliff was pacing the porch when we finally started across the bridge. He glanced up then came down the steps and met us halfway.

"We were getting worried. I was about to send McGee out to make sure you were all right, that you hadn't broken a wheel or something." He shot a glance at the angry sky. "Got us a big one blowing in."

I nodded. "Looks like it. But it's only September."

"September is not too early for a nor'wester to bury us. By the looks of it, the pass is already being dumped on." His words were accompanied with puffs of steam.

I shivered and said, "We better put the horse away and get inside." A window curtain had parted and Verna's face momentarily appeared behind the glass, disappearing the moment our eyes met. Mary had seen it too.

"I don't think it will be wise to try to make town

tonight. You can stay here, Miss Kenyon."

"Thank you, Mr. Nelson, but I really think it would be best if I left right now. I can beat the storm down the valley if I hurry."

She didn't have to say what was really preventing her from staying. Cliff understood. He grimaced and nodded.

"I will drive Mary back," I offered.

"Really, Jacob," she protested, "I can take care of myself."

"I'm sure you can. But if I don't see you safely home, I'll lay awake the next three weeks worrying about you. Anyway, Doc Perry wanted to see me before I left. This will give me a chance to do that."

She glared at me. "Well, I certainly wouldn't want you to lose any sleep on my account," she replied.

I know it hadn't been the most romantic thing to tell a woman, but then we had worked that romance stuff out of our system hours ago.

Cliff was surprised by the sharp remark, but tried not to show it. "At least come inside and get warm, and have a cup of coffee before you leave. I'll fetch some blankets to take along on the ride with you."

It wasn't what she wanted, but it was the sensible thing to do. Reluctantly, she agreed to a cup of coffee first. I went around to help her down. She brushed away my hand. "I am capable of getting off by myself," she advised me and proceeded to do so. Inside the house, the atmosphere was as threatening as it had been out in the buggy. Verna was in the kitchen, her back to us, and that's how it remained.

Cliff said to Lawrence, "Run out to the barn and

fetch Mr. Kellogg's horse and saddle. Ask Mr. McGee to please come to the house too."

The boy hurried outside while Verna prepared coffee and sandwiches, and served them in a cool, mechanical manner. She was trying to be polite. Cliff and she had obviously had words while we were away. Her attempt at graciousness came across a little wooden, but it was the effort that counted. I felt a little like a man trapped in a cage with two hungry lionesses, with Verna avoiding Mary and Mary deliberately avoiding me. But Mary was stuck with me for the next several hours, and there was little she could do about that. Afterward, who knows . . . ?

"We was starting to fret about you, Cap," McGee declared, coming in from the cold, blissfully unaware of the electricity in the air.

"So I heard," I said as easily as I was able, under the circumstances.

He took a cup of coffee from Verna and said, "Thank ya, ma'am."

"You are welcome, Mr. McGee," she answered stiffly.

"I'm driving Mary back to town. Cliff thinks we might be in for a big storm. I think he might be right."

"It do look menacing, Cap. You want me to tag along?"

"No need for that. No sense in both of us getting wet and cold—" That had been a bad choice of words. Another time and it would have gone by unnoticed, but Mary had grown a paper-thin skin. She bristled, glaring eyes burning into me. I didn't look at her, as that would only be feeding wood to the blaze, and continued, "I'll be back in a day or two. Depending on just how bad this storm turns out to be." I looked at Cliff and, keeping my voice casual so as not to raise Mary's interest, said, "I think I'll take you up on your offer to drive to Castle Rock in the buckboard. I'm not up to making the trip on horseback yet."

Cliff looked pleased. "Good, good." Then he added quickly, "It's the least I can do for you."

Mary's cup clattered upon the saucer. "I am ready to leave now," she said brusquely.

Outside, the clouds had enveloped the valley in a cold, gray shroud, spitting hard, icy pellets mixed with heavier, fluffy flakes. I erected the top bows and then stretched the canvas over them, working the fasteners around the sides and back. The snow was thickening and Cliff appeared worried. Lawrence brought my horse from the barn saddled and ready to go.

"Thanks, pard, but I think I will ride in the buggy with Mary," I said. We put the saddle, blanket, and my saddlebags behind the seat, out of the weather.

A bitter wind had begun blowing down the valley, and I was grateful that we would be driving with our backs to it, instead of into it. Cliff came from the house carrying a heavy sheepskin coat.

"You'll want this," he said handing it to me.

"Thanks." I looked at Mary. "You going to be warm enough?"

"I brought along a heavier coat, and we have blankets," she said, arranging a woolen Hudson's Bay point blanket upon her lap.

Cliff reached out a hand. "Have a safe trip, Jacob. We'll be looking for you in a couple days."

"Good-bye." I snapped the reins and turned the horse toward the bridge. As the timbers rumbled beneath us, I glanced back at the house. McGee and Lawrence were standing on the ground, Cliff had an arm around Verna's waist, standing on the porch. Cliff waved good-bye. She did not. Then the door opened and Penny stepped out clutching a shawl in front of her. She threw me a big-armed wave, and a smile. I threw one back to her. It was hard to believe she had tried to kill me. I had come to know the real Penny Nelson, the person inside her struggling to find her own way, feeling trapped in a world that no longer fitted her. How I knew that feeling. I knew that if she ever gave me a chance, I could help her with that journey . . . and maybe, I wondered, she might be able to help me with mine.

We rolled away from the house and I was torn with contrary feelings. I had grown close to this family, a thing I had avoided since the war. But at the same time I was not going to be underfoot for the next few days. There was a definite freedom in that which I longed for right now.

I was aware of Mary studying me, sitting straight and very proper in the seat beside me. Who would have thought that just a few hours ago she had tried to tempt me with her flirtations. Who'd have thought that I would have poured a bucket of cold water on the affair even before it got started. Certainly not me. And it was obvious she had not either.

I looked over. Mary averted her eyes and focused instead upon the heavy snowflakes thickening the landscape ahead of the horse. The weather was by far more worthy of her attention than the heartless dolt sitting beside her. Wasn't she worth losing three nights' sleep over? Wasn't she worth getting wet and cold for?

Apparently Mary Kenyon thought she was.

17

"THIS IS GOING to be a mighty long trip if you don't let go of that cat what's got your tongue, Mary," I said finally, when her silence had dragged on long enough. I still couldn't see what she was so all-fired angry about. I didn't figure I had done anything she herself hadn't been up to.

Mary merely brushed at the snowflakes accumulating upon her lap blanket and continued staring beyond the horse's wet back, at the veiled road ahead, as if I wasn't there. I frowned and glanced up at the sagging canvas overhead.

"Why are we stopping?" Mary demanded as I hauled back on the reins.

I grinned. "So, the pretty lady has a tongue, after all." I set the brake and dropped to the ground and began kicking aside the snow beneath a stand of ponderosa pines.

Her eyes flashed. "Don't get flip with me, Mr. Kellogg. I asked you a question."

It was *Mr. Kellogg* now. We seemed to have come far from *darling*. I should have been disturbed by it, but I wasn't. I was more intrigued by her sudden stormy-sunshine change of moods. So, this was the dark side of Mary Kenyon, I mused.

I found what I was searching for beneath the snow and dragged free a downed pine bough. "About three years ago I was up in Montana. It was a day much like this, early fall, and I was traveling to Kalispell from a place called Whitefish. I was riding in a buggy very much like this when it began to snow. Came down so fast and heavy I couldn't see but fifty feet in any direction. It was wet snow, like this," I told her, brushing it from the canvas over her head.

"Well, as it turned out, the canvas was sun-rotted along the seams. The weight of all that snow busted them wide open and filled that buggy like it was parked beneath a coal chute."

"My canvas is not rotted, Mr. Kellogg," she informed me.

"I am certain it isn't. Just the same, I'd feel better clearing it off." I finished the job, brushed the snow from my coat and climbed back onto the seat, plunging my fingers into the fleece-lined pockets.

"You should be wearing gloves." A note of concern made it past that icy exterior in spite of herself.

"Yes, ma'am."

The concern was replaced at once with her cold stare. "Serves you right, the way you have been treating me. And after I came all the way out here just to see you, Jacob."

Jacob? What had happened to *Mr. Kellogg*? Mood-

iest female I had ever met. Suddenly she was pouting.
I didn't understand it, and was tired of trying. I rum-
maged through my saddlebags for a pair of worn
leather gloves and slipped them on. Three fingertips
poked through and there was a hole in one palm, but
they were better than nothing. Mary eyed them disap-
provingly.

When I got the horse moving again, she said, "Jacob?" Her voice had softened some.

"Yes?"

She hesitated, having difficulty looking at me. "I'm
sorry. I'm afraid I've been . . ." She hesitated. "Such a
witch." She still didn't look at me, and I had to wonder
if the pink of her cheeks was from embarrassment or
just the sting of the wind.

It was the wind, I decided.

She grew uncomfortable under my gaze, fumbled for
a word, and finally blurted, "This morning you seemed
to . . . to change, Jacob. My word, your brash manners— What's so funny?" Her eyes narrowed suddenly,
glaring.

I checked my laughter. "But I told you. I was only
turning the tables, Mary. Just giving back a little of
what you were dishing out. But maybe I went a little
overboard with it."

"And that's all it was to you. Just a game?" Anger
mingled with surprise.

"A very bad game, I'm afraid. And I apologize for
it. Maybe it was because I have been so helpless for so
long that I just had to make a show of my own inde-
pendence. It just so happened that your teasing is what
set it off."

"But I wasn't . . ."

My sideways glance cut her off and her hot glare softened. Then she was laughing too. "Okay, maybe I was teasing—just a little."

It was good to see her smile again, this woman of swiftly changing moods—sort of like the weather in Cliff's valley; warm and sunny in the morning, dark, moody, cold in the afternoon. We continued on, but now that that fierce tension between us had broken, even the wind with its icy teeth seemed not quite so worrisome. But the blizzard did not lessen, shrinking the world in on us to a mere fifty feet in all directions, and it was getting darker. I dipped into my vest pocket for the watch. It was nearly seven o'clock. Penny's Indian Night had snuck up on us and overtaken us.

The events of the day boiled around inside my head, and it occurred to me that I'd only seen Penny as we were leaving, even though she had been at the house all day. Did she harbor a bitterness toward Mary too? I shook my head, marveling at the contrariness of women.

"You are frowning, Jacob."

"Am I?"

"You are still angry with me, aren't you?"

I looked over. There was that pout again, but I could tell it was only stage dressing.

"Actually, I was thinking of Penny Nelson."

Her expression hardened slightly and she turned away and stared into the swirling snow. "Penny is a little young, don't you think?"

"Not like that," I said, maybe a bit too quickly, for Mary was suddenly peering hard into my face, eyebrows knitted close, wonderment vaguely concealed behind the scowl.

"I was thinking that she had made herself scarce while you were around," I explained reasonably. "Is there any reason why Penny should want to avoid you?"

"None I can think of. But then, I'd have said the same for Verna. Is it reasonable she would consider me responsible for her tragedy because Carver once worked for me? What about Filby? Carver worked for him too."

"It goes deeper than that, Mary."

"Whatever do you mean?" A note of caution was in her voice, but I didn't think anything of it right then.

"I don't think it was you, personally, that made Verna into an iceberg."

"Then what?"

"Not a what, but a who."

Her expression went from curious to confused.

I said, "Julie."

"Julie?"

"Nothing was ever said to me, but that would be my guess."

Mary frowned at her gloved hands resting upon the wool blanket over her lap. For a moment her breathing had ceased, her breath caught and held as she considered; the steady plodding of the horses and the creak of the rig were unnaturally loud as we rolled on into the gathering gloom. Suddenly, a cloud of breath broke the silence and she said, "I won't let Julie go just because she has romantic interests in a man like Carver. She is a good worker, and her personal life is none of my business, and none of Verna's," she added sharply.

"The whole family is hurting pretty bad," I said, somehow feeling an obligation to defend the Nelsons. "I know it isn't logical, but to Verna's way of thinking, you are guilty by association."

She turned suddenly and stared. Something like concern flashed across her face. Then it was gone and once again Mary was peering into the nothingness of the coming night and the graying veil of the storm. "Penny had come into the café on several occasions, and she has never acted standoffish."

"Wonder what made a difference today." I was talking to myself, more than to her.

A gleam suddenly lit her eye, as if a great revelation had all at once made itself known to her. She started to say something, then stopped. That gleam faded, but a smirk remained in its wake, and when she spoke, she changed subjects completely. "How do you know where we are going, Jacob? I can't make out anything, let alone see where the road is."

"The road is right where it has always been. Beneath us. And your horse seems to be doing just fine following it."

"The horse is finding his own way?"

"I'm just holding onto these reins for something to do. Left up to me, we'd probably be sitting in the river right now." I grinned at her and she laughed.

Like we'd walked through a gray curtain, all at once the snow was gone. One minute we were in the midst of the blinding blizzard, and the next we rolled out under a broken sky with a pale moon looking cold behind dark clouds. The road had leveled out and the scrubby oak and open grass said this was Iron Ridge land and we had finally left the high mountains behind us. I reined in and looked back at the angry gray wall in the shifting moonlight.

Mary said, "The mountains are like that. Often there will be snow at the higher elevations before Calico Lace finally sees any."

I looked away from the gunmetal gloom that shrouded the higher reaches of the mountain and clucked the horse into motion again. It was almost eleven when we entered the main street of Calico Lace. Mary guided me through narrow side streets to a house set a few blocks off the main road.

"I live there," she said, pointing. We rolled to a stop in front of a small log building. The house was dark and looked lonely at this late hour, and Mary hesitated a moment on the seat beside me, as if weighing something on her mind. "Would you care to come in for some tea?"

"Thank you, but I think I will pass for tonight." Her invitation was tempting, for I was cold, and hungry, and I enjoyed her company—mostly. But I wanted to be by myself a while, to think through what I was truly feeling. Being too near to Mary seemed to blur my judgment.

"You aren't thinking of driving back tonight?"

"No, not tonight. And anyway, Doc Perry made me promise I'd let him check over his handiwork."

"Oh, yes, I forgot that."

"I'll just take a room at the hotel for the night."

"Will I see you tomorrow?"

I knew what she was wondering and I said, "I'll stop by the café in the morning. I should know better by then what my plans are. I might stay around for a few days."

She smiled. "Good. Will you be a dear and take the buggy around to the livery? Hiram will know what to do with it." She leaned across and gave me a quick kiss on the cheek. Before I could come around to help her, she had already lowered herself to the ground and was hurrying up the flagstone walk to her front door. She got it open, waved good-bye, and disappeared inside.

I sat there a moment after she had gone. A lamp was lighted inside and Mary's silhouette moved across the drawn curtains. She cut a fine figure of a woman. Then the shadow was gone. The time had come for some hard decision; the sort that I had been running from since the war. I shivered, and told myself it was just the cold. As I turned the buggy and started back into town, memories of Betty worked their way gently into my brain. She was always there, never far, standing as a yardstick for any other to be measured against.

Betty had been a loving wife, headstrong at times, with honest values cast in iron and the heart of a child . . . a little like Penny. It shocked me to make the comparison. I'd never been able to do that before. Betty was likely to believe in Indian Nights, or in grizzly bears forming from the shadows of rocks, when the moonlight struck them just right. She hadn't been much more than a child herself when she had died . . .

If only I had been there that night when they had

come upon the lonely farm, instead off somewhere fighting for an ideal. If I had maybe . . .

I stamped out that line of thinking. It could do no good now, so many years later.

18

I WAS SURPRISED to find someone still awake this late at night. He was a tall, spindly fellow with narrow arms and bulging eyes that, when they looked at you, made you suspect they were really seeing something at your back. The hair atop his bony skull was sparse and scattered as if he had just stepped out of a whirlwind. He turned from the stall where he had been scraping old hay into a pile with a wooden pitchfork, scrubbed his nose with his sleeve, and sniffed from the dust in the air. Then he coughed and spat and studied me a long moment in the light that spilled from the open doorway to the small room built against one of the walls.

"Howdy," I said, leading the horse and buggy deeper into the barn.

He didn't say anything at first, his face contorting from indifference to frown. When he did, his words slurred out, and the odor of whiskey came with them.

"You ain't Johnny Carver."

"No, I'm not, and mighty thankful for it." I untied my horse from the back of the buggy and lifted out my saddle and saddlebags from behind the seat. "You Hiram?"

He shook his head. "Ain't. You must be that capt'n feller the Nelson girl plugged last month." He spoke slow, as if it was difficult to form the words. His bulging eyes never wavered from my face.

Last month.

Had it been only a month? Somehow, it seemed a lot longer than that.

"Heard tell how you looked like Johnny."

"Such has been my misfortune."

He grunted and shifted his view. "That thar be Miss Kenyon's rig."

"Right again, my friend. Where is Hiram?"

"Home. Him go home for the night. Be back in the morning."

"Got a stall for my horse?"

"Reckon I do." He put aside the fork and took Mary's rig over to a rail and started undoing the traces. "Just leave your animal thar, mister. I'll tend to him soon as I finish up here."

"Where do you want me to put these?" I asked.

He waved a bony hand at a saddle tree. "Set it thar." I heaved the saddle onto the tree and put the bags across the seat. I didn't want to leave my guns unattended and buckled the holster belt around my waist. I slid the Winchester from its saddle boot. "Got a place where I can leave this?" I asked.

He eyed the rifle from among the traces and said, "You can leave it on the desk in the office. I'll lock her up for you." A crooked finger stabbed at the open door where the light was coming from. The office was cluttered, and reeked of stale whiskey. I set the Winchester among the papers scattered about. He was still working on the buggy when I came out, hitched up the collar of my coat and headed for the door.

"You was one lucky feller, Capt'n," the gaunt stableman said, bringing me around.

"How so?"

"Still alive."

"Yes, I know that."

The coot seemed like he wanted to talk. "They was like this, you know." He crossed his fingers. "That Nelson girl and her little brother. Like two peas."

"Did you know Joey Nelson?" I asked.

"Uh-huh. I know'd him. Was thar when he got hisself kilt."

"You were one of the witnesses?"

"A witness? You might say that."

"Was it a fair fight, like the sheriff was told?"

The scarecrow gave a gap-toothed grin. "Fair?" he laughed. "Oh, it were fair all right—that is, if'n you can say facing Johnny Carver is ever a fair fight. Johnny saw to it that the kid slapped leather first, only . . ." He was going to say more, but let it drop at that and turned back to Mary's horse.

"Only what?" I probed, curious now.

His fish eyes came back around to me again. He thought, then said, "It were a fair fight as far as the law calls it so, but it weren't over no gal, not like the story has it. No sir, it sure weren't over no gal."

"Tell me some more."

His narrow shoulders heaved in a show of indifference. "T'ain't no more to tell." He went back to unhitching Mary's horse.

"If not over Julie, then what?"

"Told you, mister. I don't know. I was shoveling manure in the back stalls when I hears them commence to arguing. It was harsh words they was throwing about, but I didn't follow it all. They was going on 'bout this and that. Young Nelson was jabbering something 'bout his pa, but thar weren't no words about no gal. I did hear mention of gold, though. Couldn't make out how it was fitting in to the fight they was having." He removed the traces and hung them on a peg. "Not that I'd be trying to hear something not meant for these ears. Wouldn't do that. I just work the stables and mind my own business . . . mostly."

Cold cut through the sheepskin coat as I stepped up onto the boardwalk and headed for the hotel. The old man had given me something to ponder on. But how much of it was true, and how much just feathers on a wooden duck? There was no way to tell. I turned up the collar and hunched into it, crossed the street a little farther on and put the icy wind to my back. When I came to the hotel, I strode on past. Too much on my mind for sleep, I angled through the dark toward the saloon.

A step sounded on the walk behind me. "Hold up there, mister." Something hard touched my spine. I stopped and spread my arms.

"Careful with that thing, Sheriff," I said.

"Turn around . . . real slow."

I did. Thad Griever's eyes compressed. He studied me a moment, the obvious question written across his lean face.

"Kellogg? That you?"

I grinned and he sighed, shaking his head. "It is."

"I just got over being shot once, Sheriff. I'd be obliged if you point that scattergun in some other direction."

The muzzle swung up at the dark sky and he settled the butt plate against his narrow hip. "I'd seen you coming from the livery. I wondered if it might be you, but I couldn't be sure." He peered hard at me. "Still can't be sure."

"It's me. Got a great big scar on my chest to prove it now."

He gave a short laugh. "Carver's been seen in town of late. I didn't want to take no chances . . . Him and Zeb are real chummy, you understand."

"Zeb? You mean that gaffer at the livery?"

Griever pushed out his lower lip. "It's cold chitchatting here. You was heading toward Millford's?" He didn't wait for an answer and stepped out in front of me. I followed Griever into the saloon, catching the stares from the men inside as we came through the door, letting the cold air spill in. The stove in the middle of the floor was glowing, and popping, and the odor of wood smoke mingling with coal oil lent a bit of hominess to the warm barroom. A man feeding the stove wood looked up as the heavy iron door clanked shut. There was that vague look of uncertainty in all the men's eyes, but it passed when they realized Thad and I were together.

We took a table by the wall, beneath the staircase. Thad dropped his scattergun on it, pulled back a chair, and hooked a finger at the barman.

Millford came over, and Griever said, "I'll have the usual. Make it small. I'm still working. Get Mr. Kellogg here whatever he wants."

"I'll take some brandy, if you have it."

Millford trotted back to the bar and Griever eyed me suspiciously. "Brandy?" Griever grunted his disapproval. "I can tell you've been spending time with Cliff Nelson."

I laughed.

"Ever hear of Zebedee Brant?" Griever asked.

"Can't say as I have."

"I'm not surprised. Brant was a few years before your time. About twenty years or so ago most half the states in the Union had paper out on him. But he never was caught. He was a smart one. Slippery as a catfish, and mean as a badger when cornered. Then all of a sudden Brant disappeared. He must have gone into hiding, and anyone who cared just figured the scoundrel met his rightful end. He stayed out of sight until the statute of limitations run out on him. One day about two years ago he showed up here, and has managed to keep himself out of trouble ever since."

"So?"

"So, just keep that in mind."

Millford brought over the drinks. When he left I said, "I'll remember that next time I bump into him, Sheriff." I lifted my glass to him.

He frowned, then laughed briefly and leaned back in his chair, stretching out his long legs under the table.

"You just wait, Mr. Kellogg, someday you'll be riding a rocking chair instead of a stallion . . . if you are lucky enough to make it that long."

"I sincerely hope so, Sheriff. I truly do."

The door opened. A gust of chill air swept in and with it came two men. One of them shouldered the door shut with a bang then peeled off his gloves and cupped his hands to his mouth, warming them with his breath. The second fellow, the taller of the two, spread his fingers before the stove a moment. Rubbing his hands together, he stepped to the bar. The shorter one tucked his gloves under his arm and moved to a vacant table. His partner brought a bottle and two glasses over.

"So, what brings you into town on such a disagreeable night, Mr. Kellogg?" Griever asked. "Mary find her way out to the Nelsons' place all right?"

I looked back at the sheriff. "She made it without any trouble. Fact is, that's why I'm here. I drove her back when the storm hit. There is a hell of a blizzard blowing up there."

"I'd seen it coming. A mite early in the year for our first snow, but I've a feeling we'll be digging out our front doors come morning."

Griever went on about the weather. My gaze settled upon the two men just in from the cold. I thought I had seen the shorter one before, but there had been so many new faces this last month it had become a chore to keep track of them all. He shrugged out of his coat and slung it over the back of his chair. As he came around again, the light from the smoky lamps above glinted dully off the silver conchos on his gun belt, and I remembered.

This was the man who had called to Mary from the

alleyway those two times, when she had been on her way to Doc Perry's house, bringing me breakfast. I remembered the stern look on her face each time she had left him, and I wondered what business he could have with Mary. He was a young man, in his early twenties, and he didn't seem yet to have acquired much of a need for a razor. But in spite of that, there was a self-assured cockiness about him. I could see it in the way he sat there talking with bold gestures; a strutting rooster, I decided as he stroked a match to life on the heel of his boot and put the fire to a cigar.

"Folks get a little nervous when they are being stared at," Griever said.

I dragged my eyes off the two. "Didn't realize I was staring."

"You didn't hear the last dozen words I have said, either."

I nodded at the pair. "Who are they?"

"Wranglers, far as I know. Work for Matt Stringer, on the Iron Ridge outfit. Tall one, he's Harley Smith. A friendly sort. Keeps his nose clean. He comes into town with friends now and again. Has a drink or two, does his shopping, never makes any trouble. He's a quiet sort."

"And the other?"

Griever frowned. "He's a young, show-offy kid who thinks he's a hand with a gun and a ladies' man. I don't much care for him. He's been hanging around Calico Lace four or five years now, and has been in and out of my jail more than a dozen times. Nothing serious. He's a bully when he can get away with it. I've run him in on some petty theft charges, but he's always managed to avoid going to trial. Either he has paid back what he took, or no one has come forward to press charges.

"For a while he was palling around with John Carver. Reckon that is where he caught the bug for fancy guns and leather. His name is Everett. Mason Everett."

"Mason?" I glanced back at the kid, then at Griever. The sheriff had sharp eyes. You don't grow old in his line of work without being able to read the signs, and he was reading mine plain enough.

"The name means something to you."

"Penny has been hanging around with a man named Mason." I nodded his direction. "That fellow, and Cliff doesn't like it much."

My brain began putting it all together, like the pieces of a puzzle, and I didn't like the picture it was showing me: Mason and Penny . . . Mason and Mary . . . Mary and me . . . Mary and Julie . . . Julie and Carver . . . Carver and one dead Joey Nelson. I'm not big on coincidences. One, I can accept, especially in a small place like Calico Lace. But any more than that and I start getting nervous.

Griever grunted. "Cliff Nelson seems to be a fair judge of character. Penny would be wise to listen to him."

"Told her just about the same thing, Sheriff," I said, keeping my suspicions to myself.

He shook his head. "You know how kids can be sometimes. Some just got to learn the hard way. Penny comes from a good family, and she's strong willed and sensible—mostly. She'll make out all right."

Strong willed. That was about as truthful a description of Penny as I'd heard. I was suddenly thinking of another woman who had been strong willed . . .

"Well, I best be on my way, Mr. Kellogg. Millie will be waiting up for me. She does that all the time." He grinned. "But it's kind of nice to know there is someone waiting for you who cares." He tossed down the rest of his drink and stood, cradling the scattergun in his right arm. "You staying in town awhile?"

"I'll be around most the day tomorrow. Doc wanted to check me over before I pulled out. I don't know beyond that. I'm planning to ride down to Castle Rock in a couple days to catch the train. Reckon I'll be heading back up the mountains tomorrow afternoon, or the next."

"Maybe I'll see you before you take off. If not, it was a pleasure getting to know you, Mr. Kellogg." Griever tugged his hat back onto his head. "Oh, next time you see your friend McGee, tell him howdy from an old rebel."

I laughed and said I would do that. Griever strolled off, and when the door closed behind him, I bought another brandy while Mason and Harley made headway into their bottle of whiskey.

19

NEITHER HARLEY NOR Mason paid anyone any attention when they first came in, and now, after an hour with the bottle, they no longer cared. Finally Harley Smith pushed back his chair, crawled into his heavy coat, and made his way unsteadily out the door. Mason stayed awhile longer. He finished the whiskey in his glass then spent some time peering out the front window into the blackness beyond, keeping his back toward me.

He fished a watch from his pocket, then poured himself another drink, apparently settling in for the night. I kept to myself in my corner, sipping easy at my drink to make it last. I wanted to fit in, and drinking was the best way to do that. But I didn't want to get drunk in the process.

Twenty minutes later he pulled out his watch again, popped the lid, then snapped it shut. He pushed away his glass and buttoned himself into his coat.

•   •   •

The cold sky was threatening snow. I peered back at the gray curtain sweeping down the mountainside, obscuring the moonlight, rushing headlong toward Calico Lace. Ahead of me, the small, dark figure turned a corner. I followed at a safe distance.

He started up a dark street with me keeping on his tail. Here the building acted as a windbreak against the chilling gusts. The storm had overtaken Calico Lace, and heavy, wind-driven snow pelted my cheek. Mason appeared in no hurry as he trudged against the biting wind, leaving the main street of town behind him. I kept him in sight, hanging back far enough not to be seen.

I was thinking about the pass; that it must be under several feet of snow by this time. Since this was an early storm, the snow would probably melt off before the heavier winter snows closed it down until spring. Even so, this early blizzard would still be enough to close it off for several weeks. That meant Cliff's big gold shipment would have to go by way of the valley road, across Iron Ridge land, and any deceit he hoped would lie in sending his special armor-plated wagon over the pass would be useless to him now. His plans would have to be changed.

Mason turned left, and suddenly I knew where he was heading. And for some reason, it didn't surprise me. He went up to the door and knocked. Mary's face appeared in the wedge of light that opened. She stepped aside without a word and Mason went in.

The few trees scattered about offered little cover, but at this late hour no one would be watching anyway. I sidled along the back of her house and stopped at a window.

The curtains were drawn, but a gap where they met offered a narrow view of the interior. Mason was standing there, gloves wadded in his fist, his other hand making big motions, like he had in the saloon. I could faintly hear him through the glass, but the whistling wind around the corner of the house garbled his words.

Mary had not been expecting him. She had been asleep, and now wore a faded pink robe and had that rumpled look of someone hurriedly roused from bed. Her sudden scowl told me that whatever news he brought, she didn't like it. When he finished, Mary nodded, turned on her heels, and disappeared into another room. She was back in five minutes, buttoning up a heavy sweater and reaching for a coat and scarf. When she bent toward a mirror to set a hat to her head, I backed away and waited behind the privy.

The storm had laid down a white carpet when the door finally squeaked on frozen hinges and the two of them stepped outside, bending their footsteps back toward town. I was glad to be moving again. My toes were becoming numb and my ears were afire with the cold. As before, I kept a goodly distance between us.

When they turned a corner and climbed a dark flight of back steps, I drew up and lingered at the alley's mouth. From here I had a view past a gutter downpipe of the landing where they waited in the shadow of a building. Mason knocked again, impatiently this time. A window near the door brightened with the flickering light of a lantern whose wick needed trimming. Mason fidgeted, hands tucked under his arms, shifting from foot to foot to keep warm. Mary hugged herself, her view moving warily up and down the alley. A curtain moved and a face looked out the window. A lock rattled and the door opened and quickly closed behind them.

I shivered there for a few minutes waiting, and when it became apparent no one was coming out, I left cover and mounted the steps, hunkering beside the window. As at Mary's place, a gap showed me Mason pacing back and forth across a brown and yellow carpet that covered most of the floor. He was explaining something, but the glass and the wind muffled his words. A hand flashed past and Mary pranced briefly across my view. She disappeared somewhere in the room beyond.

I waited, hearing wind sing down the alley while the cold gnawed at my toes and ears. Then the creak of a board riveted my attention. I wheeled about toward the steps and froze in mid-motion. The gun in his hand leveled, and those four distinctive clicks reached me as clear and as terrifying as the day Penny Nelson had put a gun to my chest and pulled the trigger.

It occurred to me that during my long recovery I had become careless, and that could be an unhealthy habit. Three times I had been caught off guard, and sooner or later the odds were going to turn against me. Maybe they already had. I couldn't make out his face in the shadows, but I recognized the hat—the flat brim and tall Montana Peak. It hadn't been just another nightmare. Whoever had appeared at the foot of my bed that first night had been flesh and blood, not some contrived horror of a tortured brain. He had been real, and now he was pointing a real gun at me—a shiny, nickel-plated six-shooter.

"Inside, mister," he ordered, flagging the gun at the door.

"Whatever you say." I turned the knob and pushed it open. Mason stopped his pacing and spun on his heels, hand striking snake-like for the revolver on his hip. Mary's head snapped up. Her eyes went wide and she came out of a chair. At the table, wrapped in a green silk robe, all that long, strawberry hair tied up in a loose knot, Julie Albright glared up at me. The glare shot past me then and fixed upon the man with the gun at my back.

"What is going on here?"

I didn't have to see his face to know who he was. Who else would chance sneaking into Doc Perry's house just to study me from the shadows? After all, he had heard how I looked like him, and how that had nearly gotten me killed. Well, I was curious too.

"I caught him snooping outside your window, Julie," Carver said, shoving me across the room. I stumbled and caught the edge of the table.

"Stop that!" Mary ordered. She rushed to me and gently put an arm around me, helping me up. "You all right, Jacob?" She glared at Carver. "He's still not fully recovered."

"His problem, not mine."

Mason stared at me, then at Carver. "What the hell are we gonna do with him?"

In the lamplight I managed to get a good look at my so-called twin. The resemblance was remarkable, but I'd hardly say we had both been cut from the same leather. He was several years younger than I and, although as tall as myself, leaner and lighter. Hand to hand, I'd have the advantage—that is, if I wasn't, as Mary had told him, still on the mend.

Carver said to Julie, "Check him for iron."

She found the Colt under the sheepskin coat and gave it to him.

"Well? What are we going to do with him?" Mason insisted.

I'd discovered them all together, and it was plain that this was not a late-night poetry reading club. There was something going on, something that could not bear the light of day. Carver, Mason, Julie . . . and Mary. And they were all in on it together. To me, the answer to Mason's question was as plain as the flat nose on his face. In spite of his bravado, Mason was not very smart if he had to ask.

Carver snorted. There was disgust in his voice when he had to lay it out plain for the kid. "Same thing we did the last time someone found out."

"No!" Mary cried. "You said no more. You promised."

Julie slid up alongside Carver, studying me with concern in her pale eyes. She was not so pretty now, not like I remembered her. Her face was still attractive in a freckled sort of way, but the eyes were harsh and calculating, with a glint of desperation in them. "We'll have to be careful, Johnny. He has made a lot of friends here. Nelson will be suspicious if he just up and disappears. Then there is that friend of his, McGee."

Mary stared with horror growing in her wide brown eyes. She cared . . . she really cared. I don't know why that should have surprised me. She had tried to make it plain enough.

I said to her, "What did you expect? When you start to play serious games, you need to be ready for the consequences." I glanced at Carver. "Isn't that right?"

Hard eyes bored into me. There was nothing in them that was soft, or caring. "We don't play games here, Kellogg."

"You don't?" I grinned and looked at Julie. "Well, she does. Don't you, Julie?"

She blinked, confused, and looked at Carver. "What is he talking about, Johnny?"

Carver's eyes never left me. "He's just blowing off at the mouth."

I said, "Julie played a game with Joey Nelson. A deadly game, and the kid lost." A twitch in the girl's cold, blue eyes told me I'd hit it right.

"You used him, didn't you, Julie?"

Her face grew suddenly intent.

"You used Joey to learn when the gold shipments were going out, and which ones were big enough to make it worth your while risking a holdup." I'd struck a tender nerve. "Then you'd pass the word to Mason, maybe through Mary? Mason had a habit of meeting with her at an alley near her café. Not that it couldn't have been done anytime. A café is a pretty public place. No one would suspect. Mason works for Matt Stringer. He'd be in a position to know if men were going to be working that stretch of Iron Ridge land the day Cliff was taking his gold through." Mary's face had gone rigid, and the color of flour. Julie's was fiery red. I said to her, "But something happened. Somehow Joey discovered he was being used. That's when Carver badgered him into a gunfight and killed him. It was an easy thing to blame it on jealousy. Jealousy covers a multitude of sins, doesn't it, Julie?"

"Shut up!" Mason barked.

He was feeling chesty with that six-gun close at hand, but there was something I intended to tell him, and it struck me in a more personal way than when I had spoken of Joey. My anger boiled, but my head was clear when I turned on the kid and said, "Why should I? Is it because I've touched too close to your own deception?" Suddenly I wanted to wrap my fingers around his throat and throttle that sneer off his face. "With Joey dead, you were in need of another inside man, and Penny was the only one left vulnerable enough to use. I have little respect for people who betray others, and a damn sight less for vermin who dangle the carrot of love in front of innocent young women like Penny."

I had gotten to him, and he took a menacing step toward me, confident in himself . . . in his gun. I don't know what he had in mind. Maybe he expected me to stand there while he beat me with his pistol. Maybe. But he wasn't expecting what happened next. I had forgotten the danger to myself, forgotten about Carver's shiny Colts, forgotten everything but this poor excuse of a man, and his lying betrayal of Penny. My fist shot out, and shock registered in his eyes an instant before it connected.

Mason didn't have time to reach for his gun. He threw up his arms to block the punch, but it was too late. His head snapped back and I caught the front of his shirt with my other hand and slammed him against the wall, rattling his teeth. His arms flung wide with the impact, and I hit him again just as hard as I could, feeling bone crunch beneath my knuckles. I hit him again, and again. Blood spurted, adding fuel to my fire. I was only vaguely aware of the pain that raged in my chest.

Mason feebly tried to protect himself, but I'd come on too fast, too recklessly. As he slumped beneath my raining blows, I half expected to hear Carver's gun, to feel the hot slug burn into me, ending this. But it never came. Yanking Mason away from the wall, I drove my bunched knuckles into his chin and sent him sprawling across the room. His head struck the corner of the table with a sickening thud and he slumped to the floor. He didn't move as the crimson pool thickened upon the floor, soaking his hair.

I staggered, feeling a hand reach out for me. Then Mary had an arm around me as I doubled over, vicious claws of fire raking my chest. My lungs screamed as my heart convulsed violently with throbs of sickening pain. Somehow, with Mary's help, I found a chair. My vision blurred and I tried to clear it.

"It's all right now, darling. Try to take it easy," Mary was saying. Slowly the pain subsided, and my eyes cleared. When I looked up, Mary's worried face was hovering near. Beyond it, curiously, John Carver was grinning.

"I've wanted to do that for a long time. The kid has outgrown his britches."

"Are you all right, Jacob?" Mary asked, worried eyes searching my face.

"Do you really care?" I asked, fighting down the razor fingers that clawed at my chest. I believed at that moment, like me, she really did not know.

Mary stiffened and stood. "I don't know why I should." Her voice was cool, harboring a note of hurt she couldn't quite cover. I was sorry I had said it.

"Johnny." Julie was bent over Mason. "Johnny, he's hurt real bad."

Carver put a gun into her hand. "Keep him covered." He turned the kid over and studied the ashen face, placed a finger alongside Mason's neck. A slow grin worked its way across his face and he lowered the kid back into the pool of blood. "He's hurt real bad, all right, Julie baby. He's dead."

She made a startled sound in her throat and stepped back from the body. "Now what are we going to do?" She made a wide circle around Mason's body and stood next to her boyfriend.

"I don't see how this changes our plans. If anything, him killing Mason has given us a stronger hand."

Julie looked perplexed. Carver went on, "But first we have to make sure Kellogg doesn't make any more trouble. Have you got a rope?"

She shook her head.

"There is one on my saddle. Get it."

Julie pulled a long, black coat over the shimmering green robe and went outside. Her slippered feet padded down the steps until the sound of them was lost in the wind.

Carver said to Mary, "Get Mason's gun. Don't want to leave any firearms laying around to give your friend any ideas."

Mary took the gun and gave it to him. He shoved it under his belt, with mine, then crossed to one of the chairs and sat in it, keeping me in his sights at all time. Hesitantly, Mary returned to the chair she had occupied when I first came in. We sat there a few minutes, looking at each other.

Carver stood and lifted back the curtain, looking for Julie. "What was so all-fired important that Mason had to call for this meeting? Why did it have to be tonight? Did he mention it to you?"

Mary's eyes lingered a moment on the body. "I don't know all that he had on his mind. He said something about Cliff planning a switch of some kind."

"Switch?"

She shrugged. "Something about a special gold wagon, it being a decoy, I think. There was something about lead bars and taking the pass instead of the valley road. But he wasn't specific. You know how Mason can be . . . could be. If he could keep it a mystery and make you guess, he figured he was being clever."

"Yeah, that was Mason's way. Did he happen to mention when?"

"Not straight out, but he did say the day after tomorrow was the end of it for him here, and that he was going to finally leave this wide spot in the road and kick up his heels in Denver City."

"Day after tomorrow?" Carver shook his head. "Not with the snow the pass is getting. Nothing will be going that way for weeks."

"Then what do you think Nelson will do?"

Footsteps sounded on the steps outside. Julie was returning. Carver said, "The only way Nelson is going to get his gold to Castle Rock is by the valley road. That's how he'll take it now."

A gust of icy wind ruffled the curtains. Julie quickly shoved the door shut, shivering and stamping the snow from her slipped feet. "It's coming down real hard, Johnny," she said, giving him the rope and moving close to her stove.

Carver nodded at me. "Over here, Kellogg."

The torment in my chest had eased some. I stood cautiously, wincing at a twinge deep inside, and crossed my hands behind me at his beckoning. He yanked the rope tight, the cords biting into my wrists. When he finished, he swung me around and looked me up and down, scowling.

"I still don't think he looks the least bit like me, Julie baby. He's an old man and ugly as a warty toad."

"It's only a distant resemblance, Johnny," she said warily. John Carver was not a man to upset, if you know what was good for you. And as far as it being *only a distant resemblance,* Julie did not tell him that she had gotten mighty close to me before discovering the fact herself.

He laughed. "Distant is right. About as distant as Denver City is to Calico Lace."

She laughed lightly at his joke.

He shoved me over to the table and pushed me into the chair. I winced at a stab of pain and made a note that the gent had taken one too many liberties with my body, and that if I ever got the chance, I was going to ignore my *weakened* condition and stomp the living hell out of him . . . if I ever got that chance. I took what comfort there was in that thought, and worked my hands some, urging more blood to flow past the knots he had put in the rope.

Julie was staring at the body on her floor. "We can't just leave him laying there, Johnny."

Carver sucked in a breath and studied the problem. Then he was grinning again. "I have a notion that should take care of all our problems, and not leave anyone suspicious." His view shifted, contemplating me where I sat. "Yeah, I know exactly what we are going to do."

"You're worse than Mason," Mary said impatiently, strain tightening her throat. "Stop gloating and just say it."

He cast a sideways glance at her. "I wouldn't want to trouble you with the details, Mary. I know you have a thing for this guy. Can't say that I understand it, but you do."

She hesitated, creases deepening in her forehead while growing anger hoed crow's feet at the corners of her eyes. "I don't know either," she sighed, turning from me. "I don't care what you do with him, John."

20

HE LET THE curtain fall back in place and said, "You're right, Julie baby. Snowing like all get-out. Must be near zero out there." He paused, considering, then said casually, "Wonder how long a man might survive out there, without a coat?"

Mary was pacing the floor, arms sternly folded across her waist, eyes cast down at the faded carpet. She stopped, glanced from Carver to me, then quickly looked away. I couldn't read her. She'd gone cold and indifferent toward me. Earlier, Mary had spread a sheet over Mason's body, and I had spent the last half hour watching a spot of red soak through it and spread from a point where the sheet had sagged into the pool of thickening blood.

Julie was over at the stove and poured out three cups of tea. "I don't know. An hour? Maybe two?" she replied, disinterested. "Why?"

"I was just thinking."

Mary stopped and turned on him. "Just what are you thinking, John?"

He took the cup from Julie, sipped, and made a face. "Ain't you got anything stronger than this?"

"I can brew up some coffee," she said.

"Better do it. We'll be up all night."

"John?" Mary insisted.

Carver said, "I'm thinking we take Kellogg and Mason out along the road somewhere between town and the Nelsons' place. Make it look like Mason got the jump on Kellogg while he was on his way back, see. They fought and Kellogg beat the kid real bad. But before he died, Mason managed to get off a shot. We'll put Mason's gun in his hand and arrange the bodies to look like it happened that way. If anyone asks questions, you can tell them that Kellogg had an eye for Penny, and that Mason heard of it and went after him." Carver grinned. "You know how a man can get when he see another moving in on his gal."

Mary glanced at me, then back. "Him and Penny? Who would believe it?"

I found it hard to believe myself, but when I thought it over, it struck me that of the women I had met so far in Calico Lace, only Penny had been honest enough to show on the outside what she was feeling inside. And her feeling ran deep. Deep enough to stand for what she believed was right, even if that meant shooting a man to see justice done. Penny was young, confused, impulsive, and restless, but she was honest and had the iron will to stand behind her convictions.

Verna showed that same sort of honesty, I decided, recalling her open hostility toward Mary. There was something Verna had seen, some sort of sixth sense a woman has when confronted with deception—Mary's sort of deception. I didn't understand it, and probably never would.

"He just spent three weeks with her, didn't he? No telling what might develop between a man and woman in that time. Penny is a right pretty gal, and could beguile any man."

Mary looked at me, her eyes clouding.

Julie was frowning. She didn't like the plan either, but knew enough not to cross this man. "All right, Johnny, if you think it's the best way."

"It's the only way."

Carver's plan had merit, and if it worked out it would provide a clean disposal of his two most immediate problems and keep everyone involved above suspicion. Carver was watching me, looking for some reaction. I wasn't going to give him the satisfaction, and I detected disappointment when he finally turned back to the window and lifted away the curtain again. Snow had turned the windowpane white. He let it go and said, "We'll give it another hour, just to be sure no one will see us taking him over to the livery."

"No," Mary said suddenly, stepping between the two of us.

"Too late to change your mind, Mary. We are all in on this, and we are going to see it through."

Mary was thinking fast. She said, "I'm not changing my mind." Her tongue licked quickly across her lips as she cast her eyes my way. "But you can't do it—at least not tonight."

"Why not tonight?"

"Because he told Cliff and McGee he was staying in town tonight. He said he was going to see Doc Perry first, and wouldn't plan on leaving until tomorrow afternoon, or later. If you set it up like he left tonight, especially in this weather, people are going to start to wonder why. McGee will be pounding down my door asking questions I won't be able to answer."

She was stalling for time. It was a good stab, and it might work.

Carver slammed down the cup and hovered over me, his sharp breath stinging my nose. "Is what she's saying true?" he demanded.

"You are asking me?"

His fist swung out, clipping me on the chin and driving me to the floor. I've been hit harder, but couldn't remember when. Mary rushed over and put herself between us again, helping me back to the chair.

"No more, John."

I worked my jaw. It wasn't broken. I was keeping a tally and put another mental check next to John Carver's name. The thought brought a grin to my face and that enraged him more. Mason had been the turning point, I realized. I'm of a peaceful and easygoing nature, so long as folks leave me alone. But ever since arriving in Calico Lace, I'd been in one battle after another, and I had taken about enough of it. I flexed my fingers in the ropes that held them tight, itching to wrap them around Carver's throat.

He loomed over me, raising his fist again.

"I told you the truth," Mary insisted, interceding for me. "He wasn't planning to leave until tomorrow afternoon. And all his friends know it."

"I want to hear it from him!" Carver demanded.

Getting beaten senseless by this man, with my hands tied behind my back, wasn't going to make the night pass any more pleasantly. I had already marked him for a dead man. It was only a matter of time, and of the right opportunity coming about. And when I made my move, it would take all the strength I had left within me. Strength that I needed to conserve now, so I said the words he wanted to hear.

Slowly he dropped his fist. "That's better." He stepped back, reining in his rage. "All right, we'll wait until tomorrow. But no longer."

"Tomorrow!" Julie shot out of the chair. "What the hell am I supposed to do with that . . . that *thing* until tomorrow?" She stabbed at the covered shape lying in the middle of her floor.

Carver laughed. "It's not bothering nothing."

"Get it out of here! I don't care what you do with it, just get it out of my sight!"

Carver tried to calm her. "All right, Julie baby, just settle down. I'll move it for you."

"And the carpet too," she said shaking, putting a hand to her head. "It has blood all over it. I don't want it around."

"Okay, okay. I'll take it all away. I'll stash Mason somewhere. It's cold enough that he'll keep. Fact is, it is a good idea to move him tonight. That way we'll only have Kellogg to worry about in the morning."

Julie hugged back a shiver, stared a moment at the bloody sheet, then wheeled away. "I better get dressed. It appears we are all going to be up the rest of the night."

She disappeared into another room. Without a word, Mary went back to her tea, tasted it, and made a face as she sat down again. It was clear that nobody was happy with the turn of events.

Least of all, me.

"Where did Mason leave his horse?"

"It was tied out in front of the saloon the last I saw."

"The saloon? Why the hell would he do a thing like that? Someone's surely spotted it and wondered why it's not put up by now."

Mary shrugged and flavored her words with a dash of sarcasm. "I suppose he figured he'd be getting back to it soon. Getting killed usually isn't uppermost in most folks' mind, you know."

Carver shot her a tight look. "Getting mouthy, aren't we, Mary? Someone is going to have to go get it."

"I'll go, Johnny," Julie said. "I'm getting sick of stepping around that thing." She turned a disdainful face at the lumpy sheet. "I need to get out for a while anyway," she said, buttoning herself into her coat and turning a scarf about her head and throat, tucking it inside.

When she left, Carver grinned at Mary and said, "Julie is a good kid."

Mary didn't move, her view fixed upon the wire handle of the stove door. She hadn't spoken hardly at all the last hour. Carver checked the knots on my wrists and, satisfied that they were still tight, went to the front window and watched Julie start across the street.

Mary was my only hope; my ace in the hole, but there was no way to know if she would come through for me when the time came. She had withdrawn into herself; empty eyes staring into space midway between the floor and ceiling.

Carver stayed near the window, watching the street. From my angle I could make out only a small section of it, but I knew Julie was on her way back when he swung around toward the door. A gust of icy air momentarily filled the little apartment.

"I tied his horse to the railing," she said opening her coat to the warmth of the potbelly stove.

Carver gathered Mason up in the sheet and heaved him onto his shoulder. "I'll be back later. Keep a close eye on Kellogg. If he tries anything, shoot him. For what we are going to do, we don't necessarily need him alive."

"I'll take care of things here, Johnny. You be careful." She kissed him hard, then closed the door behind him, leaning against it and giving out a long sigh. "Thank God that is over with."

Mary came out of her trance. "It doesn't bother you, does it?"

Julie pushed away from the door and went to the side table where Carver had left my revolver. "What are you talking about?"

"That Mason is dead. That we are going to kill again before this is over with. That Joey Nelson had to die . . . that doesn't seem to bother you at all."

Her laugh came short and hard, and she picked up the Colt. Studying it in the lamplight, she turned it slowly over in her hands then dropped it back onto the wooden tabletop. "Bother me?" Julie asked curiously, crossing to stare past the curtains at the dark street below. "Should it?"

Her casual tone turned suddenly angry. "It doesn't, but I'll tell you what does bother me." Julie put her back to the window, glanced briefly at me, then at Mary. "Being poor bothers me. Being a nobody bothers me. Look at this place. Nothing but a shack above an undertaker's parlor!" Her stare hardened. "The same things that bother me must bother you too, Mary, or you wouldn't be into this up to your nose with Johnny and me. Why should I care about Mason, or Joey," her view shifted, "or Kellogg for that matter . . . or anyone else. It's Johnny and me, and he cares."

"Do you really think John Carver cares about anyone but himself?"

"Shut up," she hissed, glaring at me. "What do you know about anything?"

I remembered Julie's sugarcoated sweetness that first morning. It was a startling reminder not to judge a person until I got to know them better. So much for the lesson in human character. It didn't take much to figure out Julie's motivations. Mary's, however, were a bit more complicated.

She listened quietly as Julie raged on. "After this time, Johnny and I will have plenty of money. We'll move away from here and buy us a nice place somewhere. I won't have to sweat anymore for anyone. Won't have to cook up their grub or scrape and scrub their dirty dishes afterwards with only this drab little apartment and a handful of worn dresses to show for my efforts. We'll be someone, and folks will care! We'll make them care!"

Julie finished and sulked back to the window. The snow falling silently beyond it. Her back quivered, her breathing coming in harsh and emotion-filled bursts.

Mary's empty teacup seemed to hold her full attention, her deep thoughts. She looked up from it, startled, when I spoke to her.

"And what are your reasons?"

"Reasons?" she asked softly. A pained look fled across her face. "I suppose they are very much like Julie's, as she so kindly pointed out. Greed. Not being satisfied with where I am, with *who* I am."

"People respect you, Mary. Sheriff Griever thinks the world of you."

"But I don't think the world of me," she shot back, nostrils flaring. "I want more than a greasy spoon or a friendly hello. More than old men like Thad Griever to *think the world of me*. I want to travel, to see the places a person only reads about in books—San Francisco, New York, a steamship to Europe." She gave a short, bitter laugh. "And that's more than a two-bit café in a one-horse town can give me. I wanted what Cliff Nelson's gold could buy. So I went along with them. No one was supposed to get hurt, and we figured Nelson could afford to lose a couple shipments of gold and still make out."

"But somehow Joey Nelson learned the truth." I glanced at the woman standing at the window. "The truth that he was being used to get the dates of the big gold shipments. It's smarter and safer to knock over two or three big shipments than a half dozen small ones, right?"

Julie turned from the frosted glass. Her anger past, she only frowned and spoke evenly. "It was not like you make it out, Mr. Kellogg. I never played up to Joey, not like Mason did with Penny. Joey and I were just friends, that's all. When he came to town, we'd sometimes get together. We'd talk."

"And somehow the conversation would come around to the mill, and when Cliff was sending out another large shipment?"

"It's not my fault Joey wasn't more careful who he told those kinds of things to," she snapped.

"No, I suppose not. I suspect it's just natural that a friend trusts another friend." I looked at Mary. "It's a mistake we all make at times."

Mary retreated from my stare, peering back into her empty cup. I looked back at Julie.

"So, Joey learned the truth," I went on. "How did he discover he was being played for a sucker?"

Julie stepped away from the window. "He overheard Johnny and me talking one day, out behind Hiram's Livery, where Johnny was working. Joey got mad and accused us of stealing from his pa. Johnny told me to go back to the café, and he and Joey would talk about it. Next thing I knew, they were shooting at each other. Johnny had some friends claim it was self-defense then spread the word that Joey drew down on him because he was jealous of Johnny and me." She paused by the end table and picked up the revolver again, turning it over in her hands. "I didn't like it," she said, looking at the six-shooter in her hands. Her voice grew somber. "Joey was a nice kid. We had known each other a long time. But Johnny and me, we couldn't let him discover what we were doing . . . could we, Mr. Kellogg?" she added, glancing up.

"The good die young, or so the saying goes."

"Oh, shut up!"

I looked at the red stain on her floorboards. "Well, not only the good. What about Mason? What were his reasons?"

"His reasons?" Julie crossed the room, swinging my revolver by the barrel. "Mason's reason was the same as all of ours." She cast an accusing look at Mary and made sure she saw it. "Greed. Nelson once hired Mason to ride guard on a shipment of gold. That's when he got to know the family. So when we needed someone on the inside to replace Joey, Mason was only too eager to take on the job. He had an eye for Penny, and Penny had an eye for anything in pants." Julie laughed. "It was the perfect arrangement. Mason had his cake and could eat it too. Penny was even looser with her tongue than her little brother—my word, weren't those kids ever taught how to keep a secret?"

Julie's degrading remarks irked me as she pranced across the room, swinging the revolver carelessly. Arrogant, cocksure, and not much more than a kid herself, she wasn't too old, or too sophisticated, to be above a good spanking. And if my hands had been free, she'd have found herself over my knees with her skirts over her head, howling in tempo with my hand.

She stopped abruptly and studied me. "I don't like what I'm seeing in your eyes, Kellogg." Then her face lighted. "Say, maybe Johnny is right about you. Maybe you are sweet on the girl."

"Maybe it's just that in my book, people who walk

through life on the backs of other folks are a little lower than pond scum, Miss Albright." The words sounded grand, but they rang a little too pompously in my ears. I wondered why I had said them, and curiously I was thinking of Mason, suddenly questioning why I had gone after him like I had. Could there be some truth to what Julie was saying after all?

"You're a self-righteous fool," Julie shot back, spinning on her heels. She tossed the revolver onto the table and strode across the room, banging the door to the next room shut behind her.

Mary watched after her, then slowly found my face. "Julie is right about you and Penny, isn't she?"

"I don't know." It was as honest a reply as I could give just then. I was only beginning to discover feelings that had lain dormant for too many years.

"I think you do. I think you know, but are afraid to admit it to yourself."

"Even if I did, after tomorrow it won't make much difference, will it, Mary?"

My words stung and Mary grew silent.

I tried again at the ropes, twisting my hands in them. They were tingling, and the skin, rubbed raw, burned, but my efforts were doing no good. Mary was my only hope, and I had to get through to her somehow.

I said, "She saw right through you, and I was so blind."

Her chin lifted. "Verna?"

"Her open anger puzzled me. So out of character for her. But now I see it, even if she didn't fully understand herself. And you were so insistent on your innocence, indignant at her harsh treatment. You had me fooled, Mary."

"Let's just drop it."

"Let's not." I lowered my voice. "There is no way to bring back Joey, to wash his blood from your hands. But you can stop it from happening again."

Her brown eyes went wide. "But I couldn't do what you are suggesting. They would kill me!" she whispered, glancing around.

"No, I suppose you can't . . ."

Just then the door opened and Julie came back into the room. "What time did Johnny leave?" she asked, glancing at the clock on the wall. She had changed her blouse and combed out her long, reddish hair.

"I didn't notice," Mary said softly, looking away.

Julie turned, eyebrows arching questioningly at me. I shrugged.

Her mouth tightened with impatience. "He said an hour. He should be back soon." She paced to the window to resume her vigil into the cold, snowy night. I turned briefly back to Mary, my only hope. Her eyes briefly met mine, then slanted away.

A few minutes later Mary stood and poured herself another cup of tea from the pot on the stove. When she'd finished, she stood behind Julie, watching the snow thickening upon the roof across the street. Then she returned to her chair, brushing close to the little end table near the door where Julie had left my revolver. When she had passed by, it was gone.

21

CARVER RETURNED, CHEEKS glowing, wiping a runny nose on his coat sleeve. "Got it all taken care of," he said, stamping his feet and brushing snow from his trousers. "Zeb said he'd keep Kellogg locked up in one of those back cribs he has at the livery until noon."

He and Zeb had obviously worked out some arrangement to secret me out of town after that, but Carver wasn't talking details now as he stood near the stove trying to get warm. Julie poured him a cup of coffee. He hugged it in his hands, warming them. No one spoke much, and after a few minutes they settled down to wait out the long night.

Sometime after that, I dozed off.

At a sound I came awake, lifting my head off my chest.

Carver was pacing the room, glancing out the window at each pass. He drew up, seeing me awake.

"Feel any better for the rest?"

"Not much," I said.

He gave a short, quiet laugh and stopped to peer outside. Though it was still dark, I detected a rosy, predawn glow reflecting off the snow-laden roofs across the street. The clock said it was nearly five-thirty. All but one lamp had been extinguished and the room was dark. Julie purred softly in a chair, her head cradled upon folded arms across the tabletop. So innocent, so childlike.

Mary was asleep too, curled up on the settee, looking a little like a rag doll, all rumpled and tangle-haired. She had had a long night too. Wrestling with one's conscience can be hard work.

Quickly I glanced at the end table. My revolver was still gone and, remarkably, neither Carver nor Julie had noticed. I looked away just as quickly, not wanting to give Carver anything to be suspicious about.

"You look like you're the only one here who didn't get any sleep."

"Looks that way," he replied quietly.

The sky was brightening and in its thin light John Carver looked even younger than he had the night before. I wondered how anyone could have really mistaken me for him. The resemblance was there; the shape of his face, the set of his jaw, the curve of his eyebrows. But it was only a passing likeness at best. There was no depth to it, and the more I studied, the harder it was seeing myself in his face. But then, maybe I was looking deeper than just the outward appearances.

I inclined my head at the window. "It's about time, isn't it? Before the town wakes?"

He frowned. "You in some kind of hurry to die?"

There wasn't much I could say that wouldn't have sounded corny or bold—or both—so I kept my mouth shut. I could see he was worrying about something, maybe getting me to the livery unseen, and he could see that I was right. Giving a grunt, Carver slapped his hands together and shouted, "Rise and shine, ladies. Time to get your female fannies out of the sack!"

Julie's eyes snapped open and her head leaped from her folded arms. Scowling, she combed a limp wisp of reddish hair from across her eyes and straightened up stiffly in the chair. "You could at least be a little more civilized about how you go and wake people up, Johnny."

He laughed. "What do you want, baby? A little kiss on the neck, maybe?"

Her cheeks flushed slightly, her scowl softening. "It would be a pleasant change."

"Don't hold your breath. Got no time for niceties. We got to get Kellogg on over to the livery before folks begin to crawl out of their warm beds." He shifted his attention. "You too, Mary. Crawl out of the sack and get a-moving."

Mary unfolded herself from the cramped settee, groggy-eyed, stretching like a cat coming out of a deep sleep. She stumbled for her coat, asking, "What time is it?"

"There is a clock on the wall," Carver said. "Can't you tell time?"

His rudeness set her back a notch. She regrouped, coming fully awake, and threw him a burning look that would have made old Mephistopheles break out in a hot sweat. But Carver, shrugging into his heavy coat, didn't see it. Mary glanced at the clock. "It's time already?"

"It is." There was no feeling in his blunt statement. One of those nickel-plated Colts whispered from its holster and Carver said, "On your feet, Kellogg," motioning me toward the door. He slapped my hat onto my head and prodded me through the thick sheepskin coat which I had spent the night in.

The women bundled up, and Carver ushered me toward the door. "Give me the littlest cause, mister, and I won't wait until later," he warned and the point of his revolver ground against my spine. "We are all going to walk real casual, just like nothing is wrong. Like we were all heading out for a friendly church social. Understand me?"

I nodded.

"I'll have you covered the whole way. Step one inch out of line and you can kiss the morning good-bye." He shot Mary a worried look. "What's wrong with you?"

Her eyes flashed from me to him. "Nothing. Nothing is wrong. Just get this over with, all right?"

"A little while longer. Don't go soft on me, Mary." His words held a warning, and a threat.

"I won't," she answered.

He moved me outside onto the snow-covered landing, where the wind bit hard through the coat I had worn all night. Mary and Julie went first, kicking a trail for me through eight inches of snow that hid the steps. I was more unsteady, not having the use of my hands. Though the sun had not yet mounted the sky, the snow covering made the morning appear brighter and later than it really was. Carver prodded me viciously with his revolver, and I had to wonder what sort of "church social" he had learned that from. I followed the crunch of Julie's and Mary's shoes on the frozen snow, down the alley away from the main street and turning right, onto a smaller street that ran behind a string of low buildings, half-buried by the blizzard.

The air inside the livery was as icy as it was outside. Carver rolled the heavy door shut behind us and looked quickly around.

"Zeb?" he called. "Zeb, you here?"

A horse whinnied, a hoof banged against a board. Steam from the livestock's warm breath rose like a gray cloud from the line of stable boxes. When Zeb did not appear, Carver said to Julie, "Go find that old buzzard."

She disappeared around a wall and a row of stalls. A moment after she had gone, the door to the office creaked open and the scarecrow I remembered from the night before shuffled out, slipping an arm through his suspenders.

Zeb pulled on a coat and said, "Morning, Johnny," smacking his lips, with the smell of whiskey still on his breath. "Got dumped on last night, didn't we?"

"Hurry it up," Carver said impatiently.

The old man felt around inside his coat pocket, smacked his lips again then gave a grin like an ear of Indian corn with most the kernels missing. "Guess I forgot the key, Johnny."

"Go get it!" Carver snapped, casting at the door. It would be a bad moment for someone to come for his horse just now. Zeb went back into the office while Carver grabbed my arm and pulled me toward the back of the building. We stopped at a heavy, padlocked door, Carver glancing at the big barn doors, gnawing his lips in vexation.

Mary moved close to me, huddled so deep in her coat it appeared to swallow her up. I saw her uncertainty, heard the hesitation in her voice. "I'm sorry, Jacob," she said, keeping an eye on Carver, who was staring anxiously toward the front of the barn. "I didn't want it to end this way." Her eyes found mine and the intensity I saw there told me this was more than her fond farewell sentiment. It was something else, something that terrified her. Her view went back to Carver, but he was not interested in her, her feelings, or what she was saying to me right then. Zeb would be coming any second. If Mary was having a change of heart, she had better act on it soon. I knew she carried my revolver, but it might as well have been a hundred miles away for all the good it was going to do me with my hands still tied.

Carver was still waiting for Zeb. Moving closer, Mary shot me a quick, narrow look filled with warning. Cold steel touched my wrists. It was sharp and sawed through the ropes in an instant, and the next, Mary was shoving a revolver into my blood-starved fingers. They refused to work right. I grappled at the gun.

"Johnny!" Julie had come around the end stall and was stabbing a finger at us.

He was quick.

I fumbled the revolver into position but he already had his gun out. Its barrel cracked alongside my face, spinning my head around. I staggered back. Carver's balled fist came up, rock-hard and lightning fast, and I couldn't stop it.

The dirt floor was cold against my cheek. Blood spilled from my mouth, steaming, giving up its warmth to the icy air. I was too stunned to move at once. Somewhere nearby Julie shrilled, "You traitor—you lousy traitor!"

In a dazed sort of way, I wondered why she should be getting so upset. Wasn't it the duty of the captive to try to escape? Then I realized the truth. Julie wasn't talking to me.

Zeb's voice reached me from a little ways off. "What the blazes is going on here?"

"Hurry with those keys," Carver shot back.

"She tried to help him escape. She was giving Kellogg a gun," Julie explained breathlessly.

Something like iron against iron rattled nearby. I lifted my head to try and see. Someone grabbed me under the arms and hoisted me into a cramped, dark place, too small to be called a room. Straw covered the floor, and I made out a bale or two off to one side before Carver shoved me in and swung the door. Laying there in the blackness, I heard the padlock slip back through the hasp and snap shut.

After a few seconds, their voices outside receding, I knew I wasn't alone. Her breathing gave her away . . . then her voice. "Jacob? Jacob, can you hear me?"

I was queasy in the stomach and my head was spinning. I didn't move right away, waiting for the spell to pass. There was the crush of straw when she moved, then that faint odor of perfume I remembered so well.

"Jacob?" Her voice was near my ear.

"I made a mess of that, didn't I?"

"Are you hurt badly?"

"I don't know. Don't think so." I fingered my face, feeling the blood. It seemed to be coming from a split lip. Then her hands were under my arms, dragging me to a bale of straw.

"No, it was I who made a mess of things, Jacob. I tried to help, but instead only made things worse."

"Worse for you, at least," I said, sitting. The queasiness was leaving me and my eyes were adjusting to the dark. The door, I noted, was crudely made. Wide gaps where the boards were put together allowed narrow shafts of light to filter through. I moved and put an eye to one of the gaps. Near the front of the barn, Carver and Zeb were standing at the door to the cluttered office that I remembered from the night before. They were talking but I couldn't hear their words. Julie was there too, looking worried and nervous. The monkey wrench Mary's brash action had tossed into the nicely meshing gears of their plans was making all kinds of unpleasant noises. I grinned, in spite of the hopelessness of the situation.

"What do we do now, Jacob?"

I glanced around, but could make out nothing in the dark. I tested the door. It was mounted on solid hinges and wasn't going anywhere. "Doesn't look like we can do anything but wait."

The blackness hid all but the faintest outline where she stood near the back of the tiny room.

"Wonder what this place was built for." I felt along its sides, but except for the straw, it was empty and gave no clue to what it had once held. When I peered back out the crack in the door, they were gone. I sat back on the bale and Mary slid next to me. Her neckerchief touched my face, dabbing gently at the blood there.

"The bleeding is stopping," she said.

"What made you change your mind?"

"I couldn't let them do it . . . not again. I just couldn't."

"And Joey?"

The handkerchief stopped, then she tucked it away in her pocket. "I didn't know about it until after it was over." Her deeply felt regret sounded genuine. But with Mary, I still wasn't sure. "Julie didn't know what he intended to do either. I would have tried to stop it, if I could have. Afterwards, well, it was too late to help Joey, and if I'd gone to Thad, the truth would have come out. So I just went along with it. John promised it wasn't going to happen again."

"So much for promises," I mused aloud.

The noonday sun glaring through the high windows overhead momentarily blinded me when they came back for us, pulling open the door to the dark cubbyhole. I shaded my eyes, seeing the light glint off one of John Carver's nickel-plated Colts. The barrel motioned us out of the tight room, and as my eyes adjusted, I noted Carver's dark scowl beneath the wide brim of his hat; eyes as cold and icy as the air around us. Julie stood off to one side of him, looking indignant, her arms crossed tightly in front of her. Zeb Brant had a revolver—my revolver, I noted grimly—pointed more or less in our direction, but it shook in his hand like he was a man with the palsy. His other hand gripped the reins of three horses. Mine was among them, already saddled.

"Two of 'em now," Zeb was complaining. "That complicates matters, Johnny."

"Can't be helped."

Behind them Mary's buggy had been brought around and the horse hitched into the traces. The top was still up, like I had left it. I grimaced, figuring I knew what they had planned while Mary and I were locked away. My last ride out of Calico Lace would be in that buggy. And I figured Carver would be nearby, maybe right behind the seat with a gun in my ribs. To make it work, they'd have to force Mary to do the driving. Considering the panic pulling at her face, that might be a problem. It was a look I'd seen before, in another time, another battle . . . another life. She was on the verge of snapping, and people like that sometimes do crazy things.

I nodded at the horses. "Are they the window dressing to make it look believable? Instead of just me, Penny, and Mason, now there is Mary? Your lover's triangle has just become a quadrangle." That was the surveyor in me talking, always measuring the angles. And I was looking hard for a chink in this hard box he had built around us.

"Shut up and turn around." Carver found nothing amusing in my cleverness.

I eyed the rope in his other hand and hesitated. The pistol came up. It was cocked and I weighed my chances of getting by his first shot. He had me dead in his sights and there was no way I'd avoid catching a bullet. Still, I wondered if it wouldn't be better taking my chances here and now, while still in town, than out on some lonely road someplace.

"Your hands." There was no patience left in his voice.

Reluctantly I turned, making a quick calculation. The distance to Zeb was maybe fifteen feet. More than I could cover in a single lunge, but the way the old man's hand was shaking, he'd likely put his first slug into a post. I crossed my hands behind me, thinking fast. Carver would have to put his gun away in order to tie the knots . . .

"No! You can't do this again!" Mary cried. She jumped at Carver, flinging her arms around his neck and holding on like a cocklebur in a mat of fur.

Suddenly everyone was in motion.

"Zeb!" Carver barked, grappling at her arms. But he was watching me. "Stop him, Zeb!"

I was already in motion when Zeb fired, and his bullet sizzled past my ear. His thumb hooked the hammer for a second shot about the time my fist ground against his jaw. He lurched backward, spinning about and landing in a heap.

Carver had thrown Mary aside by this time and was stabbing for a gun. I threw myself through the doorway of Zeb's cluttered office. A gun barked and the doorjamb splintered. I hit the ground hard, my chest feeling like it was being ripped apart, and rolled under the desk, papers scattering all around me. Two shots rang out, ripping the wallboards inwards and throwing splinters into the room.

I cast about for a way out, but there wasn't any. I'd

backed myself into a corner, and any second now Carver would be coming in for me, both guns chewing up everything in their way.

Then I saw it, leaning in the corner. It was the rifle I had left there last night. I scrambled for it, fingers folding through the lever even as Carver burst through, firing blindly. The place filled with gun smoke and hot lead, but I caught up the Winchester and levered a shell into its chamber.

The movement caught his eye. He spun toward me. Thunder rang in the room and something tugged at my sleeve. I lunged to the right, landing on my shoulder and swinging the rifle clumsily. Pointing one-handed, I yanked the trigger, and heard the boom as the recoil threw the butt stock back into my chin. I fought it down and worked the lever and fired again, and again.

My first bullet had caught Carver low; the second took him under the jaw, snapping his head back and kicking him out the doorway. The third had missed completely. I scrambled to my feet, levering a fresh round as I stepped through the door, hunched down low.

But Carver was no longer a worry, and the sight wasn't a pleasant one.

The sound of struggle pulled my eyes from the bloody corpse at my feet. Mary and Julie were rolling across the dirt and manure, Mary straining to keep hold of Julie's wrist. I wrenched the tiny, four-barrel Sharps pistol from her fingers then dragged the two women apart. Then Julie saw Carver. She gave a startled cry and rushed to him.

Zeb pushed himself off the floor, dazed. Before he

could regroup, I dragged the revolver out his reach with the toe of my boot and told him to stand.

He glanced at the rifle, blinked, and struggled to his feet without arguing. The side door banged open and Thad Griever turned cautiously inside, his scattergun swinging wide. He appraised the scene in a glance, his eyes dodging back and forth between Carver and myself.

"Kellogg?"

I nodded. He seemed to let go of a breath, but remained wary as an old coyote. "What happened here, Kellogg?" he demanded.

I remembered the rifle I was holding and carefully leaned it against a post. Griever eased up a bit with that. "It's a long story, Sheriff."

His view narrowed. "I want more of an explanation than that, son."

"Mary can fill you in better than I." Her face had drained of color and her feet seemed rooted near a railing where she held on with both hands, staring at what was left of John Carver's head. "In fact, I think telling it will do her good."

At that Mary looked at me, then saw the blood on my sleeve. "You've been shot."

"It's only a nick," I told her. It really wasn't more than that, and I had been growing used to bearing pain ever since I arrived here in Calico Lace.

Griever looked to Julie, bent over Carver's body and weeping. "I figured you'd find your way into mischief because of him," Griever noted.

"Not only Julie," Mary said softly.

"You?" Griever was unable to hold back his surprise.

She only nodded, and turned her eyes away.

"Never would have expected trouble from you, Mary." Thad wagged his head in disappointment and looked at me. "You all right, Kellogg?"

"I'll live."

By this time men had become to peek inside. A couple men stood around Carver's body. I grabbed up my rifle and shoved it into the saddle scabbard. Griever told a man named Horvath to go get Dr. Perry, though I didn't know why he should bother. Carver needed an undertaker, not a sawbones. I stepped into the stirrup and lifted myself gingerly onto the horse.

"Where do you think you're going, Kellogg?"

From where I sat, Mary Kenyon looked small and lonely, and Carver's body a grim reminder that, after all, I really did not like this town called Calico Lace.

Julie remained indignant and bitter to the last, glaring hatefully at me from the ground where she sat, a crumpled, ruined woman. I tried, but couldn't feel regret for her, not like I did for Mary. As I gathered up the reins into my fists, I suddenly realized that that was as far as my feeling went. Regret, and pity, and that was all.

"I'll be riding out to the Nelsons' place, Sheriff," I said, turning the horse. "There are things they need to know about what happened to Joey. And Penny will have to be told the truth about Mason . . ."

"Mason?"

In all that had happened, I had forgotten. "Somewhere between here and Cliff Nelson's place you'll find the kid's body. I don't know where exactly. I killed him, but Carver stashed him. You can get the whole story from Mary. I think she is ready to open up with a lot of what she's been carrying around inside her for months."

"Wait a minute, Kellogg. I'm going to need to hear more of this before I just let you up and ride away from here." Griever blocked my way.

"He will be back, Thad," Mary said softly with sad eyes turned up at me. "I think Jacob will be around Calico Lace for a long time."

Griever must have seen it too. Everyone seemed to know it but me. He grimaced and stepped aside. "Go on, Kellogg. Do what you have to. I know where to come looking for you if I need to."

"I'll be back," I promised, and as I turned my horse out the big double doors I thought about what Mary had said.

Jacob will be around Calico Lace for a long time.

Could she be right about that?

I didn't know yet, but as I rode out of town I discovered I was thinking about Penny, of what she needed to know, of what I could tell her. And I was thinking of Betty too, and I had a strong notion that it was time to put the past away. I'd spent a lot of years running from yesterday. Now it was time to turn my thoughts to tomorrow.

I put my horse on the road that led out of town, and as I passed the weathered sign with the flaking white painted letters, I drew to a halt.

"Calico Lace."

What kind of name was that for a town, anyway?

And maybe in the years to come I will learn the answer to that question too.